MW00438164

Death in a Time of Spanish Flu

Emily Cabot Mysteries Book 9

Frances McNamara

Rudiyat Press

ISBN: 978-1-956978-18-6 print

ISBN: 978-1-956978-19-3 ebook

For my sister Anne Marie McNamara who spent the 2020
COVID pandemic with me.

ONE

OCTOBER 12, 1918

This is madness," my husband Stephen said.

We stood at a window in a corner office of Chicago's city hall. The sill was waist high, and the window was wide and tall as the high ceilings. Outside flags waved in the hands of uniformed men getting lined up. We could hear a band practicing on the sidelines. Men unfurled banners touting the Liberty Bond drive.

"It's like there's a train barreling down the tracks towards them and they're all cheering it on," Stephen said, shaking his head. He was worried about the Spanish Flu. Our weekly meeting of the public health committee had dispersed after Stephen's unsuccessful attempt to get them to cancel the Liberty Bond parade.

He'd pleaded with them. "You've heard the report from New England," Stephen had insisted. "The hospitals there are overworked. Here, we've had over two thousand new cases and over three hundred deaths just this week. There are over three hundred thousand cases in the state outside of Chicago. The numbers are increasing every day but the only action this group has managed to agree on is to close the theaters and turn dance halls into skating rinks. Meanwhile, the saloons and churches remain open, allowing people to pass on the disease, and while the towns around the city have closed their schools, ours remain open. How can I make you understand that this disaster will be worse than the Great Chicago Fire of 1871?"

Stephen spoke as the representative of Cook County Hospital. With so many doctors and nurses gone to the war in Europe, there weren't enough to care for the sick when the epidemic hit. That was why my husband had left his laboratories at the University of Chicago to return to practice. I remembered how many years ago he had been so frustrated treating people in the slums of Philadelphia that he had come to the university to research the root causes of disease. He'd had success in research but now he was as frustrated as he was at the beginning of his career. He was fighting a losing cause trying to save people from this awful flu.

I was only an observer from Hull House at the committee meetings, so had no right to speak up. I patted his shoulder in sympathy as we looked out the window where a couple of men got into an open motorcar. Stephen snorted. "Robertson."

Dr. John Dill Robertson was the Chicago Health Commissioner. A plump fellow with a spade of a beard, he reminded me of a jellyfish. If you poked him, he'd slide away, but you had to be wary of the threads of stingers that could whip out in a painful lash. I knew that Stephen disliked the man. He was a politically minded physician appointed by the mayor. Now he was in the motorcar looking around. Hoping the mayor would join him no doubt.

Robertson had rejected Stephen's plea to close saloons and churches, saying "closing the saloons can only happen fairly if we also close the churches, and no one wants to do that."

Others on the committee were also aghast at the idea of closing houses of worship when they felt people most needed prayer. The sad truth was that churches influenced a large number of voters, and churchmen were representatives on the committee, but the saloon keepers contributed money to political campaigns. City Hall was not about to close down either type of institution. And as for the parade, my old friend Fitz had spoken up for City Hall saying, "It's too late to call off the parade now. Everyone knows it's on for this afternoon. We're terribly far behind in meeting our goal for this fourth Liberty Bond. We need the parade to raise the money we promised. We've nearly got this war won, but we have to support our troops to bring it to an end."

I was glad when Robertson ended the meeting immediately after Fitz's statement. I feared a confrontation between the representative of City Hall and Stephen who blamed Fitz for everything that had happened to our son Tommy. I'd tried to make him see he was wrong to fault Fitz but nothing I said softened his attitude. Stephen had only disdain for Fitz's point of view on anything. In a faint reflection on the window in front of me I could see Fitz coming over to us now. I stiffened.

Like my husband, Peter Francis Fitzgibbons was nearing sixty. Where Stephen was lank and balding, Fitz had become a large florid man. His red hair had turned white but was still thick on his head. He had an apologetic look on his broad open face. Stephen followed my gaze and straightened up. "I have to get back to the hospital," he said. He turned around and brushed past Fitz without a word. My old friend watched him go with a hurt look.

"I was hoping to tell Dr. Chapman I understand his argument but it's really too late to cancel the parade."

I sighed. Fitz had no idea how much my husband blamed him for Tommy's fate. I was the one who had begged Fitz to hire my youngest son at city hall. And Tommy's own actions led to his downfall. It wasn't anyone else's fault. But since our son's flight and death the previous year, I'd felt a deep well of sadness in Stephen. He blamed himself for the rift between himself and our wayward son. But that was Tommy's choice, and in the end, Stephen had tried to stand by our boy when he was in trouble. It was a wound that hadn't healed and Stephen's frustration with the flu epidemic only deepened the sore.

"Stephen had to rush back to the hospital," I told Fitz. "With so many doctors and nurses off at the war, he's gone back to practicing."

"And the influenza makes it worse, I know," Fitz said. He grimaced as if he were somehow responsible for the epidemic. Of course, he wasn't. For all the political maneuvering he'd done over the years, Fitz was always concerned with protecting the people he represented, in his own way.

"It's a crisis already, Fitz. And Stephen's certain it's going to get worse."

"These are difficult times." He looked sadder and older than I had ever seen him. He gave me a small grin and perked up a bit. "May I escort you to the reception for the Aviator Gold Star Mothers at the Fine Arts Building? They're gathering before the parade as many of them will be walking in it. You could too if you like."

I looked down, juggling my purse as I put on my gloves. I had no intention of walking in the parade, and I would have avoided the reception if I could.

After his arrest, my son Tommy had run away to France to join the Lafayette squad of aviators under a fake name. When he died in a crash the previous winter, Fitz corrected the records to make sure the authorities designated me a Gold Star Mother. He hoped to soothe my grief, although he knew I was a pacifist before America entered the war. I found the honor bitter, but Fitz would never understand that.

Two

F itz led me to a waiting automobile. I couldn't avoid the Gold Star Mothers reception without hurting his feelings, so I stifled my own and went along. As we were driven south on Michigan Avenue he shifted uncomfortably in his seat, like a guilty child.

"What is it, Fitz?" I hoped he wouldn't insist I walk in the parade. I wouldn't do that, not even to spare my old friend's feelings.

"I wanted to ask you for a favor." He looked away as he said it.

"What is it? You know I'm grateful for all you tried to do to help Tommy. I owe you for that." But I really couldn't walk in that parade. Stephen would be livid.

He moaned at my son's name. "Oh, it's a sorry thing but I need your help if you will." He turned his large body to face me. "It's Whitey. I need you to help me deal with him."

Whitey? He meant my police detective friend, Henry Whitbread. No one dared to use the nickname except Fitz.

Fitz's face reddened, and his brow furrowed. He'd often been at odds with Detective Whitbread over the years. Whitbread was my mentor and even though he had arrested my son, he and his wife, Gracie, remained friends of ours. Unlike many in his profession, Whitbread supported academic studies in criminology. We had worked together to establish cooperation between the Chicago Police Department and the University of Chicago where I taught. My students worked with Whitbread every day to compile and study statistics on crime in the city.

"How are you involved with Detective Whitbread now?" I asked Fitz.

"It's the Flora Murphy case." Fitz bit his lip as he watched me for a reaction.

"Flora Murphy? You mean the young wife of Big Mike Murphy who was arrested for shooting a man?" Despite all the intense drama of a war in Europe, where the Allies were finally winning victories, and the influenza raging at home, there was room in the papers for a scandalous story about the shooting death of a young man in a downtown office building.

Fitz seemed relieved I knew about the case. "It's a terrible tragedy all around. They're saying the young man was in love with Flora, a married woman, and it looks like she rejected him, then he shot himself in front of her. But when the police arrived, she was in shock. She'd collapsed beside him, and they took her into custody. It's a terrible mess."

"Does Whitbread think it was really Flora who shot him?" Details had been sparse in the newspaper accounts, and I hadn't paid much attention.

"Actually, he's convinced Big Mike Murphy had the boy killed."

Big Mike was the wealthy owner of gambling halls and saloons, who controlled most of the downtown wards when it came to voting. Flora was his second wife, much younger than his first, from what I'd read.

Fitz continued. "You know how Whitey gets when he's got a bug about something. There's no proof Murphy was involved. The district attorney brought Flora up for arraignment. But she's ill with shock. The judge will convene court in her prison hospital room tomorrow. She's a victim, not a villain, Emily."

"Yet Whitbread's charged her?" Whitbread was the most competent detective in the city, so I already had doubts about Fitz's story. What was he up to? Why did he want me to placate Whitbread?

"Not exactly. When Whitey was stubborn as an ox about wanting to pursue Murphy, police authorities took him off the case. They charged Flora instead. He's not happy about it. I'm afraid he'll go off half-cocked. Please, will you attend the proceedings with me? Whitbread will be there. I know you can talk some sense into him. It's a horrible ordeal for the poor woman."

"You think she's being charged to stop the investigation of Big Mike? I suppose he's an ally of your boss, the mayor?" I'd lived in Chicago long enough to know how favors worked. I wondered if Big Mike was pressuring City Hall to influence the trial.

"Oh!" Fitz writhed in agony. "It's a terrible, terrible thing. I know you'll be able to sympathize with the poor woman. Whitey is just out to get Murphy because he has pull. But Flora is the one who's hurt by all this. You can see how unfair that is, can't you? If we could get Whitey to back off his crusade against Murphy, there wouldn't be so much pressure to indict Flora."

He looked deeply distressed. I wondered if his concern was more for the woman than her powerful husband. A bachelor, Fitz was prey to romanticized feelings for women. Stephen might not appreciate what Fitz had tried to do for us, but I knew he'd done it for me. It gave him a pull on my heart. "I can come," I conceded. "But you know I can't promise to influence Henry Whitbread. If he's determined to pursue Mike Murphy, he will."

THREE

I allowed Fitz to guide me to the Gold Star Aviator
Mothers reception but as soon as he turned his back,
I managed to slip away. I wasn't surprised to see another
woman follow me out. I was fine with those women who
found comfort in such public recognition for our sons, but
it only made me sad. I saw the same sadness in the eyes of
the other woman who pursed her lips and nodded before
turning away.

I had no use for the Liberty Bond parade either. Wearing
my mask to guard against the influenza, I skirted the
crowds on Michigan Avenue, head lowered. Stephen was
right, this was no time for large gatherings. The disease
was an invisible enemy hunting among the crowds. I was
afraid of it. At the train station I chose an open-air car,
as Stephen had told me to do. In one of the steps to try
to reduce infections the trains reserved a few cars with
windows jammed open.

At home in Hyde Park, our townhouse was unnaturally
quiet. Our housekeeper, Delia, had gone to help her cousin
care for several boarders who had come down with the flu.

Stephen was still at the county hospital, where he would probably stay overnight. My oldest son, Jack, was absent. After two years as an army doctor, Jack was sent home from the front. While mostly recovered from a wound in his leg, he still hadn't returned to work as a doctor. I worried that he drank too much, but Stephen said that only time would cure him and to leave him alone.

My daughter, Lizzie, wasn't home either. She was apprenticed to Lorenzo Taft, a prominent sculptor at the Art Institute, and spent most of her time in his studio. Like her brother, she also kept late nights. After her best friend was killed, and her own engagement called off, Lizzie had retreated from her social circles. She steadily withdrew from the high society she'd previously allowed to rule her life. Since I'd encouraged her to break free of that circle of friends, I suppressed my worries about her avant-garde lifestyle, if that was what it was. I didn't know. My children no longer confided in me. When I complained of that, my husband reminded me that they were no longer children.

Feeling chilled and alone, I took a cup of tea into Stephen's study and lit a fire in the fireplace. I felt safe there. I knew whatever happened, my little family would always come together. We still mourned our youngest son, Tommy, but at last this terrible war seemed to be coming to an end. If only we could survive the encroaching epidemic that threatened everything, we could finally take up our lives again. I said a prayer for all the men still on the battlefield and for my lost son, before I stumbled up to bed. I'd promised Fitz to be present early in the morning for the arraignment of Flora Murphy.

Four

S tephen hadn't returned by the time I left home the next morning. I caught an early train and, at the Harrison Street Police Station, I checked on my students working in Detective Whitbread's office. Fitz had just arrived to escort me to the hearing when Whitbread barreled through the door.

"Fitzgibbons," he said, glaring at the City Hall man, as he hung his overcoat on a stand. Whitbread was over sixty, but you wouldn't guess it from the way he moved his tall, lanky frame. He was always in a hurry. His long face was sharply featured with deep lines. His thick mustache and sparse hair had been gray for many years. He narrowed his eyes as he considered Fitz who groaned softly even before Whitbread spoke. "You and your chums at City Hall are responsible for the chief taking the Graham investigation away from me, aren't you?"

"Now, Whitey, you know it's your commissioner who doles out your assignments. The mayor has nothing to do with it."

Whitbread snorted. I knew he hated the nickname Fitz insisted on using, but the big Irishman was oblivious to the detective's disdain. Fitz had more important people to please.

Whitbread leaned forward till he was nose to nose with the politician. "You can't protect Murphy forever. He had a hand in the death of Louis Graham, and you know it. You're offering up Flora Murphy as a sacrificial lamb because you think a jury of men will sympathize and let her off the hook. You should be ashamed of yourselves."

Fitz backed into the door and had nowhere else to retreat. He sighed and glanced at me as if to say, *you see what I have to deal with.*

I cleared my throat. "Mr. Fitzgibbons told me the hearing will be in the prison hospital, upstairs. It's such an unusual proceeding, he thought I might like to attend," I said. It was partly true. If City Hall was really protecting Big Mike, I certainly didn't sympathize, but I knew Whitbread's clashes with authority had cost him dearly in the past. I was more concerned with preventing my old friend from shooting himself in the foot than with helping Fitzgibbons.

Whitbread backed away from Fitz. "It certainly is unusual, but then everything about this case is unusual. A woman walks into a downtown office in the middle of the day and a young man is shot to death."

"Or shoots himself," Fitz insisted.

Whitbread grunted. "Where the gun came from, who else was present, the reason for the action—all these circumstances are ignored in a rush to charge a woman who immediately collapses in grief." He looked at me.

"They want to get it over with to cover up what really happened."

Fitz frowned. "That's not true. That's exactly why they removed you from the case. You just assume something nefarious involving Mike Murphy is at the root of this and it's not. It's just a tragic affair that ended in grief. You'll see. Come, Mrs. Chapman. They'll be starting soon."

Fitz ushered me upstairs to the prison hospital. Whitbread trudged along behind us. We entered a door with iron bars on the window. Inside were six hospital beds, only one of which was occupied. The patient was Flora Murphy. A wide space had been cleared to the left of the iron bedstead. Fitz and I joined a circle of people waiting there. Detective Whitbread took up a stance leaning his back against the wall with his arms crossed. The judge, wearing a black robe, sat in the only chair. He held a notepad in his lap.

A handsome older man in an expensive suit stepped to the middle of the space and spoke. "We propose that the preliminary hearing be omitted, and the case bound over for trial."

"Motion denied," the judge proclaimed.

"But, your honor, my client is ill, mentally and physically."

"Quite, Colonel Willis, which is why we have moved the hearing to the defendant since she was unable to come to us."

I saw the judge glance over at a man hovering on the opposite side of the bed. I guessed this was the famous Big Mike Murphy. He was a big man, over six feet tall with broad shoulders and a shock of thick white hair. The carved wrinkles of his face showed his age to be in his sixties. A nurse in starched cap and apron stood at his elbow.

The prosecutor stepped forward as Colonel Willis, the defense attorney, stepped back, shaking his head. They argued back and forth until the prosecutor finally called a witness. "You are Mr. Malcolm Murphy?" the prosecutor asked.

I had to strain my neck to see the stocky young man facing him who answered, "I am." A comparison of his features with those of the gambling king made it clear this was his son.

"You were one of the first to reach the office after the shot was fired at Mr. Louis Graham?"

There was a moan from the hospital bed. "Why is it, oh God, tell me what it means."

I had to stand on tiptoe, peering over a man's shoulder, to see the pale face on the pillow as the nurse stroked her forehead and hushed her. Flora Murphy was a young woman, in her twenties, I thought. Her blonde curls spread out on the pillow.

The prosecutor continued questioning Malcolm. "And before the shot was fired, did you hear anything?"

"I was in my office on the sixth floor, above them. I heard someone say, 'You don't dare. You don't dare.'"

"Was it the voice of a man or a woman?"

I saw the witness look at his father. "It was a woman's voice."

I wondered whether the father blamed the son for testifying against his stepmother. It was obvious from the pain on Big Mike's face that he cared deeply for the young woman who moved restlessly in the bed.

He looked terribly sad. He didn't look at his son. I wondered if Whitbread was right. Perhaps Malcolm omitted mentioning his father's men at the scene of the crime. Was he part of a cover up to hide Big Mike's involvement?

They called a second witness, a man from a building across the street. He replaced Malcolm opposite the prosecutor and testified that he saw figures standing at the window before the shot was fired. I noticed a little rustle went through the bystanders. He couldn't say he saw the gun fired but he saw Flora Murphy arguing with Louis Graham just before the shot.

The proceedings were soon completed. The judge held over the prisoner, Flora Murphy, for trial for the murder of Louis Graham. In a move that caused Detective Whitbread to straighten up from the wall and raise an eyebrow, the judge granted bail for five thousand dollars and dismissed us.

As we turned away, a woman's voice screeched from the doorway, "Murderer. You killed Lou."

The circle of male figures drew back from this outburst, and an older woman thrust herself forward. Flora Murphy on the bed murmured and began to raise herself from the pillow, but the nurse and Big Mike pressed her back gently. People in front of me parted for a young woman in black who took the older woman by the elbow to lead her back to the door. "Come, Mama. This is not the place."

"You killed Lou. You killed him!" The older woman strained to look back at the figure on the bed, but her daughter forced her along.

"The dead man's mother and sister," Fitz whispered in my ear.

Behind the two women, hovering in the doorway, I saw my son Jack.

FIVE

I s that your son I see with the grieving family?"
Whitbread asked.

Fitz had moved away in the crowd of men between me
and my son. Jack and the two women hurried to an elevator
and the doors closed before I reached them. I bit my lip.
What was he doing here?

"Emily?" Whitbread asked.

I shook my head. "Yes, that's Jack, but I don't know why
he's here."

A young man in a Panama hat, with a small mustache
and bright eyes, popped up at my elbow. "Excuse me,
ma'am. I'm Hecht from the *Daily News*. I noticed you were
the only female in the room besides the defendant and
the nurse until the dead man's mother appeared. What
do you think about what you heard in there today? Do
you believe the judge is right to hold Mrs. Flora Murphy
for the murder? As a woman, what do you think of a wife
who takes a younger man as a lover and then shoots him?"
He held a notebook in his hand and pulled a pencil from
behind his ear, grinning as he waited for a reply.

"Shall we return to my office?" Whitbread asked, elbowing by the newspaper reporter. I had sympathy for the young man. My brother had been a reporter in Chicago when he was younger. Hecht's questions were outrageous, but I thought I could handle him. Whitbread rolled his eyes when he saw I might engage with this representative of the press, and he turned on his heel to leave without me.

Hecht tried to follow him. "Detective Whitbread, is it true you've been taken off the case? Can you tell us why? Is City Hall influenced by Flora's husband? What did you want to investigate that led them to give you the boot?"

Whitbread waved him away and the young man turned back to me. He was eager as a puppy. I tried to distract him by telling him how my students worked with the police compiling statistics on crime. He dutifully wrote it all down, but he shivered with anticipation of something meatier to report. "Since you work with Detective Whitbread, do you know why he was taken off the Flora Murphy case?"

I sighed. "Sorry, no. My younger brother used to be a reporter in Chicago," I told him in another attempt to deflect the questions. "But he left to write screenplays for the movies."

Hecht looked up with interest. "Did he? I had an offer to get involved with the movies but my colleagues on the *News* convinced me moviemaking is a flash in the pan and I'd be a horse's ass, excuse my French, to get involved. How's he doing?"

"He seems to be having some success," I told him.

"If you'll excuse me, I see a free telephone and I need to get this story in to my editor." He pushed past a man who was leaving to reach for one of three phones on a table in the corridor. Soon he was dictating, "'You killed Lou' the dead man's mother exclaimed when the hearing of Flora Murphy for the murder of Louis Graham concluded with indictment at the prison hospital today..."

I smiled at the enthusiasm of the young reporter for the sleazy story of the gambling king's wife and her young lover. He reminded me of my brother, Alden. Glad to escape his questions, I hurried down the stairs to catch up with Whitbread. At his office I dismissed my students so I could talk to him in private.

"So now you've seen a trial moved to the prison hospital. Is that really what brought you to the scene? Or do you have a more personal interest?" he asked.

I didn't want to admit my reason for attending the trial was to try to protect Whitbread himself from his own worst impulses, "I had no idea my son would be there, if that's what you mean. Of course, I've seen trials before, but I've never witnessed a scene like that one." We stood opposite each other with his desk in between. Whitbread fixed me with his eagle-eyed stare and waited. I couldn't lie to him. "Fitz asked me to come," I admitted. "He knew you were removed from the case, and he expected you to protest. He wanted me to try to get you to temper your response, I think." As if I or anyone else could control Whitbread when he had a righteous cause. Fitz was naive to expect results. Whitbread waved off Fitz as a topic.

"Did you know the coroner's jury refused to call it murder? There was an eight-hour deadlock until they finally stated they were unable to determine whether the fatal wound was self-inflicted. The DA's office had to prosecute anyhow because of the publicity. City Hall would have been happier with self-inflicted."

Whitbread stood beside his desk with his arms extended in front of him. "It was a wound to the chest. Not easy to do to yourself." He mimed working a trigger on an imaginary gun pointed at himself. "Suicide is unlikely. Not a viable solution. That's why the authorities have to go for a conviction even if it's against the interests of Big Mike."

"Surely the authorities wouldn't try to hide the truth?"

"They shouldn't, Emily. But, as you know, the great god Graft holds sway over much that should be beyond his reach. You and I believe the Law ought to be exempt, but it is only with unsleeping diligence that we can keep our most prized freedoms." Whitbread had always hated graft. He, himself, was immune to political influence. His incorruptible integrity was one reason I'd been glad to have my students work with him. While his phrasing was often pompous, I knew his dedication to his principles was sincere.

"You think there may be improper influence at work in this trial?" I asked, thinking of Fitz.

"They calculate the distraught woman will get sympathy from a jury. More sympathy than her husband for sure. Did you see the prosecutor when the witness from across the street testified? At first, the defense lawyers tried to say it was suicide but now they're basing their case on Graham having struggled with Mrs. Murphy when he was shot by her. The prosecutors won't be able to destroy the argument if the defense can prove there was a struggle. If he were standing still and she aimed at him, she couldn't have fired the killing shot."

I was very confused by this statement. "The witness said the victim was standing, but you're saying if he really was standing still Mrs. Murphy couldn't have shot him?"

"It's the angle of the shot. It's unlikely given their respective heights." Once again miming the action, Whitbread pulled out a chair and sighted down an imaginary gun at an imaginary victim. "If he was sitting it would work. Wait and see. When they get the medical examiner on the stand, the defense will have a field day proving she couldn't have shot him on purpose."

"But you think someone else could have done it?"

"Someone much taller than Flora Murphy could have—one of Murphy's henchmen, for instance. The politicians don't want her convicted; they just want to keep Big Mike out of it. Men like Mike Murphy expect to have their way. They deal in power. But women are their downfall. Women refuse to grant them the unfailing obedience and loyalty they demand of their followers. Men like Mike Murphy are brought down by the women in their lives. Murphy certainly proved this in the choice of his first wife."

"He was married before?"

"Oh, yes. The young man who testified is the fruit of his first marriage and an unhappy one it was."

"The current Mrs. Murphy appears to be rather younger than her husband."

Whitbread motioned me to a chair and sat down behind his desk. "For years after the divorce he didn't remarry. But then he met Mrs. Flora Biggs. She was married to Kenny Biggs who ran a saloon that Big Mike owned. She was only twenty-two when Big Mike met her, and he was in his fifties. He was smitten, totally smitten."

"What about her husband?"

"What could he do? He worked for Big Mike. Kenny divorced her and now he owns the saloon. Big Mike gave her clothes, jewels, a big house in Oak Park, things beyond her dreams. They've been married eleven years." She was older than I had thought, then—over thirty.

"But she had an affair with Louis Graham?"

"Apparently. He was only twenty-three when he died. They were neighbors, out in Oak Park. He grew up on the same block as the Murphy mansion."

"So, he seduced Flora Murphy?"

"And what do you think a man like Big Mike would do about that?"

Fitz was right. Whitbread suspected Murphy. "You think he killed Graham?"

Detective Whitbread merely raised an eyebrow. "A man like that seldom does his own dirty work."

"But now he's letting his wife take the blame?" I asked. "How awful. Why wouldn't she say so if someone else killed Louis Graham? Even if it was one of her husband's men? Do you think she's afraid of what he would do to her?"

Whitbread shrugged his shoulders enigmatically.

"You don't think the young man could have taken his own life? Is that what she claims?"

"As you saw, she was fairly incoherent. It's not clear what she saw. But the angle is a difficulty." Again, he held his arms awkwardly as if pointing a gun at himself. "It seems Mr. Graham's mother doesn't believe he killed himself."

Whitbread let his arms drop to the desk. "Perhaps your son could shed light on that strong belief?"

I didn't want to admit how little I knew of my son's activities these days. "I'm not personally acquainted with Louis Graham or his family," I told him.

"I see. Well, Miss Agnes Graham, the victim's sister, is an artist, I believe," Whitbread said, then stared at me with anticipation.

"Perhaps she knows Lizzie. She's studying sculpture at the Art Institute." Whitbread obviously knew that already. He watched me with speculation. I remembered Fitz's request to get Whitbread off his hobbyhorse of Big Mike as the villain. "If Big Mike had been involved, wouldn't the witnesses have seen signs of a third person in the room?"

"Difficult to say. I believe they may even convene the court at the office in the Monadnock Building where this happened to clarify the situation. After they swear in a jury, of course. That might help to illuminate the circumstances. Mrs. Murphy is already provided with one of the most expensive defense lawyers." Whitbread's eyes narrowed and he looked grim. "In addition to trying to prove Mrs. Murphy innocent, I have no doubt the defense will try to knock down any theory that a third person was involved."

"To prove Big Mike wasn't involved?"

"He has a lot of influence and a lot of power," Whitbread said. "Like your friend Fitzgibbons, for instance." Whitbread raised his eyebrows, waiting for a reaction from me. I had none and lowered my eyes to the desktop. I couldn't defend Fitz's concern for the gambling hall owner. "Perhaps you might ask your children about

Louis Graham?" Whitbread had a spark in his eye. He was turning the tables on me.

"Of course, if they have any information of use, I'll send them to the authorities," I said. "But weren't you removed from the case?" I knew he wouldn't want to admit it. If Jack had any relevant information, I should take him to the detective in charge of the case. Would it be a betrayal of my old friend? Still, I really didn't want to encourage Whitbread to violate orders from his superiors. He'd come close to losing his job before.

Whitbread's face suffused with red. "Yes. City Hall had me removed. They'll do anything to protect Murphy, that's all. But the truth will come out in the end. They may keep me from the formal investigation, but I'll sniff out the truth despite them."

I knew from long association that it was fruitless to try to muzzle Whitbread once he had a scent. My only hope was to try to keep him from outright insubordination. To do that, I needed to keep an eye on the investigation myself. And I was uneasy about my son Jack's involvement. "Do you plan to attend when the trial visits the death scene?" I asked. "I would like to see that. Could I go?" It would be a way to keep my finger on the pulse of the investigation.

"Yes, I'll be sure to let you know when it's going to happen." There was a cold glint of interest in his eyes. I realized that he would use me to stay in touch with the case. If my son was involved, of course I would be interested. I hoped my son wasn't involved.

Six

I left Whitbread increasingly worried about my son Jack. I never saw him these days, so, I sought out the one person who might know what he was doing at that hearing with the dead man's mother and sister.

My daughter Lizzie was enrolled at the School of the Art Institute, but most days she worked in the Midway Studios of Lorenzo Taft. The famous sculptor had established his workplace in a group of buildings on Sixtieth Street beside the long stretch of green lawn left over from the Columbian Exposition. It was still called the Midway. When I returned to Hyde Park that day, I went looking for my daughter in one of the ivy-covered brick buildings that made up the studio.

It was a crisp fall day with luminous sunshine shining through red and yellow leaves. I shuffled through a brown layer of fallen leaves to the dark green door of the studio. It was quiet inside as I followed corridors to the room where I knew Lizzie worked.

"Mother, what are you doing here?" She glanced up when she heard me. Lizzie looked so different now from the time before the war, when she dressed in the latest fashions. She wore a shapeless gown that hung like a sack and had many pockets. A cotton apron was tied over it and her hair was chopped off in a daring style. But she looked happy as she bent over a clay statue she was modeling.

"I haven't visited for quite a while," I said, removing my mask since the room was empty of other people. "What are you working on?"

"It's a part of Mr. Taft's Fountain of Time. He's due back soon and he wrote instructions for the parts we should model in life size while he's away." As a wartime duty, Lorenzo Taft had been enlisted by the YMCA to go to France as a lecturer. The huge sculpture was commissioned before the war, and he had left behind a twenty-foot model. He had divvied up the main figures in the sculpture for his students to sculpt while he was gone.

"Will you sculpt it in marble after he returns?" I asked. Lizzie was working on a full-scale figure of a woman leaning toward two young boys, with an arm extended as if to protect them. The lively children seemed engrossed in play and unaware of anything around them. The faces were meant to be generalized but the tilt of the heads and the hand gestures reminded me of my own sons, Tommy and Jack, when they were boys. I swallowed to hide a sigh of recognition. I wasn't sure how Lizzie would feel about what I thought I saw in her work.

"I don't know," Lizzie said. Her head was down as she smoothed a turn of the woman's collar. "There's doubt about whether the Ferguson Trust wants to pay for the Georgia marble. I guess Mr. Taft will have to deal with that when he comes back."

"It certainly is huge." I walked over to the wall where a sketch of the full statue was taped up. "There are so many figures."

"One hundred in all," Lizzie said. "There'll be a figure of time, an old man alone opposite the full sculpture. He'll be looking at this long wave of people. Here's my group." She came over to point out the three figures in the long stream. "It's from a poem called "The Paradox of Time." See, below, they've put the quote: 'Time goes you say? Ah, no! Alas, Time stays, we go.'"

"I'm not sure I like that," I said. Considering the daily lists of the war dead and the victims of the influenza, I found the idea of the Fountain of Time disconcerting.

"True to life, though," Lizzie said. "But, Mother, did you really come to check on the progress of Taft's sculpture?" She raised an eyebrow, coaxing me to tell her what was on my mind. My daughter had become much more sensitive to my thoughts and feelings in the past year in a way that surprised me. I still thought of her as my little girl that I should take care of.

I told her about the hearing I'd witnessed in the jail, and how I glimpsed Jack leaving with the dead man's family. "He's so secretive about where he goes and what he does these days," I complained. "But he seemed to be escorting a Miss Agnes Graham and her mother. Whitbread told me she's an artist. Do you know her?"

Lizzie walked back to her clay model. "Yes, I know Agnes. It was so sad to hear about her brother Louis. Very sad."

"Did you know him, too?"

She stared off into a corner. Light filtered in from a skylight, trembling a bit from leaves that encroached on the edges. "Poor Louis. He was so unhappy lately." She turned to me. "Agnes is a friend of mine. I introduced her to Jack, and we used to go out together, Agnes, Louis, Jack and me."

My children knew the dead man. They must have been aware of the whole sordid story of Louis and Flora. They'd never mentioned it to me. "Louis Graham's mother accused Flora Murphy of killing him, but others think he killed himself," I told her. "Mr. Fitzgibbons believes he killed himself, but he's afraid the police will blame Flora's husband."

"Big Mike? Louis worked for him. In fact, they say Big Mike got Louis out of the draft. He gave him a job and sent him to California for a while. He did as much for Louis as for his own son, Malcolm."

"You know Malcolm Murphy too?" I was surprised and worried. Whitbread guessed that my children were connected to the death of Louis Graham. I didn't want them to be pulled into the whirlpool of a murder trial. I knew from experience it could be horrible. Jack still hadn't recovered from what he'd seen as a doctor at the front and Lizzie had only just regained her balance after the murder of her closest friend and the broken engagement that followed.

Lizzie sensed my concern. "It's all right, Mother. Jack and I just know Malcolm Murphy in passing. Agnes is a pretty good friend. Like me, she turned away from expectations that she'd marry to follow her heart. She's a new friend. We're all treading water till this war is over, and now this epidemic. When we get together, we pass the time and try to forget the present. No one knows what the future will bring, so no one wants to make plans. We're just existing. Anyhow, you don't have to worry about Jack and me. We'll be all right."

I was touched by her concern for me, but I wasn't reassured. "I never see Jack anymore. Half the time he doesn't even come home at night. He can't seem to go back to medicine. He isn't interested in any of the groups I work with. I can't help worrying about him."

Lizzie bit her lip. "He has a friend he stays with sometimes. Someone he knew from France."

"Why won't he bring his friend into the family? Why don't I know about him?"

"I think Jack is working with him." At my surprise she rushed to explain. "I think they didn't want to worry you. His friend was a surgeon, but now he does autopsies in the morgue at County."

"Autopsies. Wouldn't that be awfully depressing for Jack after all he's seen in the war? Is that really what he should be doing?"

"I don't know. But Father knows about it."

Stephen knew that Jack was working in the morgue of his own hospital, but he hadn't told me. My heart sank. What was going on with my children? After the death of my youngest, I couldn't bear to lose Jack or Lizzie. Or Stephen.

SEVEN

B y the next morning neither my husband nor my son
had returned. I wanted to ask Jack what he was doing
at Flora Murphy's hearing. I was determined to find and
talk to him.

Lizzie was quiet during breakfast, but she insisted on
coming to the hospital with me. We took an early train.

Cook County Hospital sat in the center of the city and
took in any sick person, no matter whether they could pay
or not. It was one of the primary teaching hospitals in the
country and the physical building had been rebuilt a few
years previously. It was a huge stone pile that filled an
entire city block. Because of the flu epidemic it was full to
bursting.

I brushed through the front door, followed by Lizzie, to
ask for Stephen at the main desk. A nurse directed us to
a flu ward and warned us to secure our masks and not to
touch anything. We trotted down corridors jammed with
stretchers along the walls. I smelled bleach and ammonia
through my cotton mask. Stephen had told me the wards
were filling up, but I hadn't imagined the numbers of sick.

When I saw people lined up like helpless lambs, I felt my
stomach drop with dread and tasted the tinny flavor of fear
in the back of my mouth. This was so much worse than the
mere numbers printed in the committee reports. A sudden
vivid memory of laying out the dead body of a young girl
during a smallpox epidemic many years ago rose in my
mind. So much death. Not again.

I heard Lizzie behind me catch her breath as we turned
into Stephen's ward. He huddled over a nurse who was
bathing the brow of a young man. Swathed in a heavy white
apron, a wide mask, gloves, and even a cap, my husband
looked like a medieval monk or an angel of final judgment.
I tapped him on the shoulder.

"Emily, what are you doing here?" He plucked the white
mask from his face to talk to us. His brow creased with
worry. "You shouldn't be here."

I wanted to be angry with him for hiding our son's doings,
but how could I be upset with him when he was working in
such a dangerous place? "Jack," I said. "Lizzie told me he's
working here, doing autopsies. Do you really thing that's
wise, Stephen? After all he's been through? And how could
you not tell me?"

His eyes rolled toward the ceiling as if in prayer. "I'm
sorry, dear. We didn't want to worry you." Grabbing my
forearm, he led me to the doorway. Lizzie trailed behind.
"He's working with Dr. Eli Lieberman. Jack knows him
from the front in France. Dr. Lieberman has been asked
to run the morgue in the emergency."

"In the morgue, Stephen? Jack's working in the morgue?"
I pulled down my mask to speak clearly. "How could you
allow it, after all he's been through?"

"He's a doctor, Emily. He can't face losing patients after all the men he lost on the front but working with Lieberman he doesn't risk that."

"Because they're already dead?" I was appalled.

"He's a grown man, Emily. Neither of us has any say in what he does."

I was furious with Stephen. How thoughtless could he be? "Where is Jack? He hasn't been home for days."

Stephen sighed. "He's in the morgue. They're very busy. Look around. You can see how desperate it is."

"Yes, well, he's not so busy he couldn't turn up at the prison hospital where Flora Murphy was charged with the murder of Louis Graham," I blurted out. Did Stephen know about that?

"What?" Obviously, he had no idea. It was so like my husband to think he knew all about our children when he didn't have the slightest clue.

"I want to see Jack."

"All right, all right. I'll take you down." He replaced his mask and turned away, knowing argument was futile when I was this upset.

We took an elevator down into the bowels of the building. It was much quieter there, where shroud-covered stretchers lined the corridors. Stephen pulled open doors to a large, cold laboratory but it was empty of living bodies. Only corpses were visible under white sheets.

"They'll be in Lieberman's office," he promised, leading the way again.

Finally, he turned into the open door of a good-sized room with high windows looking out on sidewalks. Bookshelves and filing cabinets filled one wall. A desk sat in one corner, but most of the space was filled with wide tables holding tools and other mechanical utensils. I hardly noticed those things when I entered because hanging from the opposite wall and from the ceiling were tens of legs, arms, hands. They swung gently from a breeze when Stephen opened the door. My son Jack sat in the middle of the room on a stool and beside him crouched a big dark-haired bear of a man in a huge white lab coat. Dr. Eli Lieberman.

EIGHT

"Mother," Jack said, as he looked up in surprise.

Stephen pulled down his mask. "Jack, your mother wants to talk to you." He noticed how I was staring at the arms and legs hanging like tools in a shed. "Emily, Dr. Lieberman works with amputees. Those are artificial limbs he creates and fits for his patients. Since the pandemic, he's been drafted to help with the autopsies—there are so many. Now, I have to get back to my living patients." With that he turned on his heel and left. I was sure he was glad to escape us, leaving the family drama behind him.

Dr. Lieberman rose, watching as Lizzie and I continued to stare at the hanging limbs. He grinned at our reaction. He was older than Jack, probably in his late thirties, and had dark heavy brows, a clean-shaven square face, and unruly frizzled hair in need of a cut. He used his left hand to raise his stiff right arm to show a lifeless frozen hand at the end. "I have a personal interest in artificial limbs, as you can see." His injury must have destroyed his career as a surgeon.

I felt a pang of sympathy. I couldn't help remembering the shotgun blast that had ended Stephen's career as a surgeon. That incident had happened in a West Side tenement, not a battlefield. But it had driven my husband to research at the university when he could no longer operate. Before that incident Stephen had still helped in clinics in the poor areas of the city. Jack must have seen the similarity. Perhaps he'd taken his wounded friend to Stephen to help him recover from the life changing injury.

Jack brushed past Lieberman. "Mother, Lizzie, Eli and I are helping in the morgue. As Father said, they're overwhelmed. Here, sit down." He pulled out a couple of stools so that we could sit opposite Dr. Lieberman. Tools and several artificial legs littered the broad tabletop. "We're just on a break from the autopsies." He went back to the other side of the table.

"I'm sorry to interrupt, Dr. Lieberman," I said, "but I must talk to my son in private. Could you give us a few minutes?"

He cocked an eyebrow at Jack, apparently amused to see his friend in trouble with his mother. I was embarrassing Jack, but I didn't care. "This is my office, Mrs. Chapman. I'm not prepared to leave my own office so you can scold Jack here." He smiled. "You're welcome to go next door. No one will hear you there."

"Don't be rude, Eli," Jack said. "He means the morgue. We're not going to discuss anything surrounded by corpses. Honestly." He shook his head. "What is it, Mother?"

I wasn't going to let Lieberman get my goat. "What were you doing at the prison hospital yesterday?"

Jack looked down. He'd seen me in the doorway. He must have expected the question.

"I escorted Miss Graham and her mother to the hearing. That's all. I don't see why it concerns you."

I felt like growling. It was a scandalous murder trial, and he didn't see why I should be concerned. "You saw me there with Whitbread and Fitz. Why did you ignore me?"

"I'm sorry, but it seemed more important to help Agnes get her mother away. We had no idea she would speak out like that."

Dr. Lieberman sat back comfortably, watching Jack and me as if he were at a tennis match. Meanwhile, Lizzie slid one of the artificial legs over and was examining it as if we weren't embroiled in an argument right in front of her. I was annoyed.

"How well do you know the Grahams? Lizzie tells me you socialized with the victim and his sister."

Jack glanced at Lizzie, but she resolutely turned over the leg. "Yes, they're friends. Of course, when her brother died, I told Agnes how sorry I was to hear about Louis and offered to help in any way I could. Imagine how awful it is for her mother to lose her only son and then hear the Murphy's claim it was suicide. They're telling people that Flora Murphy struggled with him to get the gun away because he was trying to shoot himself. Agnes and her mother know he would never do that. Surely you sympathize with such a terrible loss, Mother."

I felt a sharp pain. Jack was purposely calling up the memory of Tommy's death. Fitz wanted me to sympathize with Flora Murphy because she was a woman. Now, Jack expected me to sympathize with Mrs. Graham because I was a mother who had lost a son, too. But I wanted to protect my own living children. I couldn't sympathize with other women's losses of sons or lovers when I was worried that my children were being pulled into the scandal of a murder trial.

"The way Louis Graham died is under dispute," I told them. "There are powerful forces at work in this case. Detective Whitbread believes Mike Murphy might be behind the death, while Fitz represents City Hall by promoting the idea that the young man shot himself. Big Mike will fight the accusations against Flora. He has plenty of money to hire the best lawyers and plenty of influence to make the decision go his way. It's a very dangerous situation. Whitbread asked me if you or Lizzie were involved. I need to make sure that you're not."

Jack glanced at Lizzie again. What were they up to? "We're not. I have no idea who shot Louis Graham." He looked down and fiddled with a small hammer that lay on the table.

At his side, Lieberman shrugged. "Tell her," he said.

My heart thudded. "Tell me what?"

"Oh, really," Jack said. "I was in the building when Graham was shot. Or on my way out. I'd been talking to Malcolm Murphy in his office before it happened. I heard the shot on my way downstairs, but I didn't see anything."

Malcolm Murphy—Big Mike's son who testified that he heard the shot from his office upstairs and had been the first to find Flora collapsed beside the dead man. "Why were you meeting Malcolm Murphy?" I demanded.

Jack looked at Lizzie, but she ignored him again, turning over the artificial leg in her hands. Jack huffed. "It has nothing to do with Louis Graham's death."

I jammed my teeth together to prevent myself from yelling at him. What was he hiding? I wasn't sure I wanted to force him to tell me in front of Lieberman.

Lizzie finally spoke. "You really could articulate the ankle better," she said to Lieberman.

He raised his furry eyebrows. "You're an expert, are you?" He seemed amused by her obvious ploy to change the subject and egged her on.

She smiled sweetly. "I am an expert—of a sort. I'm a sculptor. I study the human body to reproduce it."

Lieberman stood, then lumbered around the table to take the leg from Lizzie's hand. She stood to face him. He balanced the artificial limb against his own lifeless right hand. "Perhaps you'd like to make me a better one? We take all the contributions we can get here. I've got a list of men waiting for prostheses." He put the leg down and considered her with a stare. "Have we met before?"

Lizzie held her ground, staring him in the eye. "I don't think so."

He shook his head. "I'm sure we have. I know...at the Dil."

I wondered what place or group he was referring to, but my children seemed to know it. It was another indication of how little I knew about their lives.

Lizzie hesitated, glancing across at Jack. "Maybe."

Jack spoke up. "Mother, I'm sorry if you're worried for us. But don't be. Eli and I should get back to work now. Please."

I preferred to have it out with him in private. "We can discuss it at home tonight."

Jack shook his head. "I'm sorry but I'm staying in town with Eli these days."

"Jack..."

"Mother, please. I have a right to make my own decisions. I'm helping with the autopsies, and I'll continue to do so while this epidemic is such an emergency. We can discuss other matters when this is all over."

Lizzie turned and took my elbow. "He's right, Mother. We should go and let them work." She nodded to Jack, ignoring Lieberman as she pulled me to the door.

It was useless to argue, so I let her lead me through the maze of corridors and stairways to the lobby. Out on the street, she said she had a class at the Art Institute and refused to join me for lunch. She hurried off. I stood still and watched her retreating figure.

I was uneasy with what I'd learned. I couldn't let it go even if I knew Jack was right, and I had to allow him to lead his life without interference from me. I stood, hesitating, looking back and forth between Cook County Hospital and my daughter's retreating back.

Finally, I turned toward the Harrison Street police station. I would spend a few hours with my students in Whitbread's office. Then, knowing the class Lizzie was attending, I intended to be there when she left the Art Institute. I'd just be careful that she didn't see me. My son and daughter were concealing something from me, and I was determined to find out what. Besides, I dreaded returning to an empty house again. Stephen was swamped with patients, and he'd never leave the hospital tonight.

NINE

B efore leaving Whitbread's office, I borrowed an old overcoat and beret from the store of disguises that he kept on hand. I should have felt foolish, but it satisfied an urge in me to be doing something I might have done in my younger days. Although my children made me feel old, I could still do the unexpected.

I stood across the street from the Art Institute at five. A few minutes later, I followed Lizzie and another young woman art student as they walked, took a trolley, and ended up in the section of the city called Towertown, north of the river. I wasn't surprised to find them headed there. It was an area where former mansions fell into disrepair and were broken up and rented out to artists, writers, and other young people with ambitions. I saw small cafes, coffee shops, and bookstores on every block.

Lizzie parted ways with her friend at a rooming house and ran up the steps of another converted brownstone. I got a coffee across the street while I waited. Soon she came out with another young woman who carried a rectangular parcel wrapped in brown paper. I thought she might be Agnes Graham.

I followed them to Washington Park, across from the Newberry Library, where smatterings of people gathered in front of speakers standing on soapboxes. At that time, people called an insane asylum a "bughouse." Nicknamed "Bughouse Square," Washington Park was a bastion of free speech. With so many speakers dotted around the park, standing on soapboxes or anything to raise them above the crowd, the cacophony could have been the noise of an asylum.

My daughter and her friend hurried past a man with a tiny following bombastically bemoaning his lack of funds in an attempt to get fifty cents for his dinner. The next group listened to a man proclaiming the health benefits of free love and a lively sex life. Someone in the audience challenged him, waving a book in his hand. The heckler claimed he'd rushed across to the Newberry Library to find a quote from Sigmund Freud to refute the speaker.

I skirted that crowd and walked through a line of benches where men sat cross legged reading newspapers in the failing light. The air was crisp, and I was glad for the extra layer of warmth provided by the overcoat. Lizzie and Agnes stopped by a crowd surrounding an animated speaker who wore a felt hat and a flowing Windsor tie. He described a hypothetical hobo woman he called Boxcar Bertha. I recognized him as Dr. Ben Reitman, well known for his work among prostitutes. At one time he was imprisoned for promoting contraception. He described "Boxcar Bertha" as a "sister of the road," a young woman who traveled around the country for free by hiding in empty train cars with other hoboes. Bertha's mother was an unmarried woman who spurned convention and had children by several men. Bertha was another free spirit who made her way by her wits, stealing or prostituting herself as necessary.

Reitman's work was familiar to people in my circles of social workers and labor activists. A natural showman, he prided himself on going further and wilder than others who bucked society's conventions. I was curious to see that my daughter and her friend were so interested in him. Lizzie had grown up knowing about the social work I studied and worked in, but I thought she had turned away from society towards the aesthetics of art as her only concern. Yet here she was with her friend listening to Reitman.

I walked by while Lizzie and Agnes's backs were turned and joined a crowd further on. A number of the speakers were members of the Industrial Workers of the World, also known as the IWW or the "Wobblies," who had unionized industries across the West. They were a revolutionary group tied to socialists and anarchists. In a dramatic raid earlier that year, most of their leaders had been jailed, charged with interfering with the draft. Anti-capitalist ravings were the meat of their rousing speeches. While I met many of these people in my work, I had no idea my children had been exposed to such radicals. In a place like Bughouse Square, they were unavoidable, and Lizzie seemed quite at home here. Why was I surprised? A chasm had grown between me and my children. I knew in my heart it was due to the numbness I had felt ever since Tommy's death. I'd let Lizzie and Jack drift away from me.

I stopped by a crowd listening to a man who claimed to be a maharajah talking about his mystical travels. Pulling my beret down, I peered back at Lizzie and saw that Jack had joined her. I swirled back to the speaker as they came toward me. Jack took the large brown paper-wrapped package from Lizzie's friend, then held her elbow. Lizzie followed, looking off into the distance as if she expected someone else to join them.

I waited till they were half a block away, then followed. They rounded a corner. By the time I reached it, they were gone from sight. I looked up and down the street. A few people hurried along home to their suppers. In the fading dusk, I noticed a green light filtering through a gap between two buildings. I sidled up and looked through to a brick alley with rubbish bins and an orange door. Straining to see, I took a hesitant step between the dirty buildings. A hand shot out and grabbed my arm pulling me through the narrow gap.

TEN

M other, did you follow us?" Lizzie demanded.
 We were in a filthy alley with rubbish scattered on the ground beside the brick walls. Jack and Lizzie's friend looked at me. As I'd guessed, it was Agnes Graham. I recognized her from when she'd led her grieving mother out of the prison ward. Now, she clutched Jack's arm. Perhaps she was more Jack's friend than Lizzie's, after all.

"You've been hiding something from me," I said. "I was worried."

I expected an art exhibition or even a dance hall, illegally open during the epidemic. Instead we were in a dirty alley. A bare green lightbulb shone above a door painted orange with "CAUTION" stenciled above it. Black lettering on the door said, "Step high, Stoop low, Leave your dignity outside."

"What is this place?" I asked. I must have looked alarmed.

"Don't worry," Agnes said. "I'm sure it's not nearly as bad as you imagine, Mrs. Chapman. Come along and you'll see." She urged Jack on, and he held the door open for us.

We had to duck down to get through a doorway made for midgets.

Inside, we were in a big barn of a place. A man rushed past us on his way out. He was being chased by a tall figure in a flowing robe, who wore a skeleton mask under his hood, and cried, "Out, out," as he thrust a pitchfork at the retreating figure. "No coughing, spitting, sneezing. Out!"

When the door slammed shut the hooded man wheeled on us. "Do you bring infection?"

"No," Jack said. "We're all healthy. I promise you. I'm a doctor."

The cloaked figure turned away as another man with thick bushy hair, long arms, and short legs stomped up to us. His pale blue eyes were slightly crossed.

"Hello, Jones," Agnes said. "We've come to hear the speakers, and I've brought you this in lieu of a quarter to get in." She prodded Jack to unwrap the brown paper from the package he carried. It turned out to be an oil painting.

While they haggled, I looked around. A huge room to the left held brightly painted chairs and benches set in a semi-circle around a stage. Paintings and drawings hung on the walls, blobs of colors or shaded cubes with a few clumsy nudes sprinkled throughout. Directly in front of me, in a smaller room, people sipped from coffee mugs and ate sandwiches.

With the epidemic raging, I didn't feel comfortable in a space crowded with people, but the high ceilings made it feel spacious. Although the men and women scattered around had shoved their masks down or stuffed them into their pockets, there were so few of them spread across two rooms that I felt safe enough.

I saw Dr. Lieberman hunched over a mug beside a longhaired man with a wide brimmed hat and flowing scarf. When I turned back to our party, I saw Agnes staring at a table on the other side of the room. I recognized Malcolm Murphy. Connected in my mind to the death of Louis Graham and the trial of Flora Murphy, I was surprised to see both Agnes and Malcolm in this unusual space. And I was even more surprised that my son and daughter seemed so accustomed to the place.

Malcolm sat in conversation with a girl who had blonde ringlets, topped by a chirpy little hat with butterflies. Two other men at the table had their backs to us. I wondered what Agnes found so fascinating. She bit her lip and returned her attention to my son and Jones, reaching across to shift the canvas my son held to horizontal. The blocks of color made a bit more sense in that position. I got the impression of a lake with trees and boats, but it was a primitive depiction.

"There. You'll take it, won't you?" Agnes asked. "Oh, Mrs. Chapman, this is Mr. Jack Jones. He runs the club. Jones, this is my Jack's mother." I heard the proprietary tone that confirmed my belief that Agnes was Jack's friend more than Lizzie's. How was it that we had never met before?

Jack Jones grinned, still slightly cockeyed, and when he reached out a hand, I saw he was missing two middle fingers. I shook it, ignoring the defect. "How do you do, Mr. Jones. I believe you know Miss Addams of Hull House. She's a friend of mine." I recognized his name as a well-known labor agitator and soapbox orator. I'd heard a rumor that he knew how to handle nitroglycerine and had lost the fingers either blowing safes or making a bomb for a labor uprising.

"Miss Addams, of course. She spoke to us last month. Welcome to the Dil Pickle." He waved an arm at the unorthodox place then took a step closer. "Are you a nut about anything? Don't you want to talk to the Picklers?"

ELEVEN

I stepped back, slightly alarmed. Would I be forced to speak in this public place? My son stuck his hand in front of Jones. "Here's three quarters for my mother, my sister, and me. Agnes is using her picture for entrance. Thanks, Jones. We'll just get coffee and sandwiches before the main event, shall we?" He took my elbow and steered me away.

"Enjoy," Jones called after us, laughing at my lack of composure.

Jack took me to Lieberman's table, where the doctor introduced us to a Mr. Sherwood Anderson, the man with the wide-brimmed hat, and a woman artist friend of his, then Jack went to get refreshments.

Lizzie explained this was my first visit to the Dil Pickle.

Anderson doffed his hat. "Welcome. I see you met Jack Jones, father, mother, and ringmaster of the Dil Pickle. That's 'Dil' with one el, by the way. Jones wanted to avoid trademark disputes." He motioned to the tables around us. "Here you'll find the streetcar conductor sits on a bench beside the college professor, the literary critic, the earnest young wife who hungers for culture, and the hobo. Jack Jones and the Dil Pickle are two bright spots in the rather somber aspect of our town. Even in the current plague." He clapped his hat to his chest and nodded his head.

"They come for the lectures," Lizzie said, ignoring Anderson's dramatics. "Of course, there are fewer people these days with the influenza."

Jack placed a tray on the table and passed around cups and saucers to the ladies and a thick mug for himself. Beside him, Lieberman produced a silver flask. "Want some?" he asked after tipping liquid into his own mug then Jack's.

I declined but Lizzie pushed her saucer forward in quiet defiance. I worried about my son's drinking and now I wondered if Lieberman was a good influence. Apparently not. Yet by accepting their behavior without criticism and even joining them, Lizzie was managing to keep on Jack's good side while he avoided me. It reassured me that Agnes refused the liquor.

Agnes looked at something over my shoulder. She stiffened. Malcolm Murphy strolled toward us. The curly haired blonde was gone, but the two other men from his table flanked him. Lizzie buried her nose in her cup.

"Invaders ahoy," Sherwood Anderson said with a grin.

"Lizzie Chapman!" Malcolm smiled. "I thought that was you. I was just talking to Jones over there about a partnership." He seemed pleased with himself. "Don't know if you've met my friends, Sean Riley and Frank Cervone."

Riley was a broad-shouldered Irishman with muttonchop sideburns. Cervone had very dark curly hair parted in the middle and slicked down with hair oil, and a bushy mustache. I remembered with a shiver Whitbread's speculation that Big Mike could have had Louis Graham killed for courting his wife. These men seemed just the type who could do something like that. They were silent but stuck to Malcolm's side like bodyguards. I wondered what Agnes Graham was thinking.

"Malcolm," Agnes said coolly. "Is your father looking to buy the Pickle now?"

Sherwood Anderson laughed. "Not likely. Jones is a teetotaler. The Pickle is no saloon. The hoboes here couldn't afford it if it was."

"We're negotiating," Malcolm said. He doffed his hat to Agnes. "So sorry about your brother. It's strange for us all to be here without him, isn't it?" He produced his own flask and added a dollop to his mug. "Here's to Louis, may he finally rest in peace."

Silence met the toast, before conversation broke out again. I thought it must be difficult for Agnes to hear her brother's name, but why was she out in public so soon after her brother's death? She steadied herself by leaning against my son.

Eli Lieberman had left the table. I wondered how he had disappeared so suddenly. We were a strange group. Malcolm turned all his attention on my daughter, complimenting her on her coat and necklace. He ignored me. I was uncomfortable with the way they all addressed each other by first name and failed to even introduce me. It was "Lizzie" this and "Agnes" that. My children's generation embraced a familiarity that seemed dangerous to me. Malcolm Murphy, with his diamond cufflinks and camel's hair coat was going out of his way to charm my daughter but his attentions slid off her as if she were made of ice. I remembered occasions in the past when I'd seen a particularly nosey woman corner Lizzie at a society function. The same glassy eyes and plastered smile reassured me that she was not taking Malcolm any more seriously than she had taken such women.

Jack became impatient. "The show's about to begin. Shall we find seats in the hall?" he said. When Jack attempted to usher both me and Lizzie into the next room, Malcolm cut in to take Lizzie's arm.

"You don't need all that brotherly protection now, do you, Lizzie?" he asked as he led her into the lecture hall. Jack growled.

"Where's Miss Graham?" I asked, reluctant to sink into the habit of using first names.

"She has something to attend to," Jack said. "Malcolm can be a bore sometimes."

I wanted to ask Jack about how well he and Lizzie had known poor Louis Graham, but not in public. I sat down on a chair between Sherwood Anderson and Lizzie, with Malcolm on her other side. The dark-haired bodyguard, Cervone, had split off and disappeared on entering the big hall. The big Irishman took a seat just behind us. Jack walked away, presumably to find Agnes. There were undercurrents here that I didn't understand.

TWELVE

We'd barely sat down when Lizzie jumped up and, waving, called out, "Milly, Milly!" She caught the attention of a young woman in the aisle and pushed past Malcolm to greet her. They put their heads together and walked down the aisle deep in conversation.

Malcolm grunted beside me and then said, "I've got business with Jones when he's off the stage." He left, signaling his Irishman to stay behind.

Voices rumbled. People stamped their feet, and someone yelled out, "What's the stall?"

"Hang on. Here we go," Anderson said.

On the stage, Jack Jones introduced the first speaker of the night as a lady from the Anti-Cigarette League. The woman spoke about the evils and pitfalls of the nicotine vice. The woman plowed on with her statistics and dire warnings.

When she reached a break, one man stood up and said loudly, "I never smoked a cigarette in my life. I've always been a snuff user. But after hearin' this woman and lookin' into her face I'm gonna start smoking. Has anybody got a cigarette?"

The crowd threw hoots and cheers and cigarettes at the man.

"You'll regret it," the woman told him.

Another man stood up and told her she was ugly enough to scare Christ off the cross.

"If only it's enough to save you from the cigarette," she exclaimed and the crowd cheered her, banging their feet. The room was as noisy as a union meeting during a strike vote. Apparently heckling was the main sport and entertainment of the place.

I looked up at the wall hung with so many paintings. In the summer of 1900, I had the opportunity to travel to Paris where I met Mary Cassatt and her friend Edgar Degas. I was not knowledgeable about art, but I knew that when Degas and others began painting in an impressionist style their paintings were considered revolutionary. Yet the pictures my friend Mary Cassatt painted drew you into a world away from the present. The pictures hanging at the Dil Pickle burst out on the world as if they would escape their frames, as if a gash in reality had been torn to let them through. I wasn't sure what to think about them. A few were more appealing than the others. I was attracted to several depicting Negro figures, leaning back and forward, dancing. They weren't realistic. Warm bright colors were outlined in heavy black. But they conveyed a joy lacking in the other paintings.

Most of the pictures and drawings seemed brutal. Did this represent the world as my children saw it? Between the war and the raging epidemic it was a harsh world out there.

With a pang of regret, I wished for Stephen's presence. He would have called me back from such bleak musings. I thought that he would like the irreverence of the Dil Pickle. He would have found the staunch refusal to glorify war and patriotism a positive response to the Liberty Bond parades and other demonstrations of recent days.

A tap on my shoulder startled me out of my reverie, as the audience clapped for the speaker. "Hello, there. We meet again."

THIRTEEN

The reporter Hecht grinned when I jumped. He shoved his chair beside me by pushing Anderson's away. "I see you've met Swatty." He slapped Anderson on his back. "Sherwood Anderson, renowned author of *Winesburg, Ohio*." The man pulled away from Hecht and looked down his nose at him. Hecht grinned.

"But here comes our Orpheus." He pointed to the stage where a banjo player was playing "Won't You Come Home Bill Bailey" while a tall man shuffled slowly across to a folding chair. "His name's Sandburg. Wait till you hear him," the enthusiastic young reporter told me.

Carl Sandburg had straight blond hair that flopped on his forehead as he leaned forward, looking up from under a furrowed brow. If I hadn't been told he was a poet, I'd have taken him for an old farmer. He moved slowly and wore creased trousers and old-fashioned boots tied up with string. He had a deep voice that stirred something in my heartstrings when he recited:

"Hog Butcher for the World,
Tool Maker, Stacker of Wheat..."

I couldn't help paying attention to a voice full of pauses and with a hint of underlying anger. Sandburg held the crowd as he described the "City of Big Shoulders." An earsplitting ovation and drumming of feet followed his performance.

I took the opportunity to stand and move around, as the evening was ending. Lizzie returned in time to hear Sherwood Anderson invite people back to his place on Cass Street for a reading. Several other young women joined a growing circle of admirers, so I moved back. My reporter friend moved with me.

"Swatty is quite a draw for the ladies," Hecht told me. "Come along and you'll see him in action." When I looked skeptical, he grinned. "Not taken in?" He glanced at the group around Anderson. "Did you know he owned a factory in Ohio, but he left it and his wife and kids? He arrived in Chicago on foot with a shaggy beard and uncertain about his identity. A victim of amnesia, apparently. Wouldn't you know he landed a job with one of the biggest ad agencies in town. His inability to remember his name stamped him as a genius in his employer's mind so he got a salary bigger than anyone else writing copy. What a life!"

"He's a friend of yours?" I asked pointedly.

Hecht beamed. "Oh, don't get me wrong. We're buddies. But I don't believe the stories he tells—none of them. He's just a great salesman, so I love to hear him talk. Come to Cass Street, and you'll see what I mean."

I declined and turned away from the rambunctious young man. I was tired. I beckoned to Lizzie. "We need to leave for the last train," I told her. I hoped to finally speak to her in private on the way home.

She frowned. "I'm not coming. I'm spending the night with Milly. We're going to Sherwood's place. Jack can take you to the station. He's around here somewhere."

She was deliberately avoiding me, and it made me angry. "Nonsense," I said. "I'm perfectly capable of getting to the station." It was true. Lord knew there were numberless nights I had returned home late from meetings without any escort. I was not happy that Jack had disappeared so completely, but I refused to let my children treat me like an elderly relative. I stood up.

"I'm sorry," Lizzie said, but it was too late.

"Never mind." I shoved my arms into my coat and pulled on my gloves. "I'll see you tomorrow, perhaps?"

I could see she felt guilty. It served her right. As I walked to the door, I thought of going to Cook County Hospital. I longed to see my husband. I knew he'd calm my anger and my fears. But he'd hate that I risked infection by showing up there.

Frigid air leaked into my mask as I pushed the door open and ducked through. The green light made a circle in the dirty alley. I looked for the narrow walkway between buildings we had used to get there. I would find a taxi on Dearborn Street.

A boot lay on the ground by a trash can. It looked like one my son wore. He had disappeared a while ago. My heart clenched and I couldn't breathe. Jack. I fell to my knees beside a man's body curled up in pain. Slicked down black curls meant it wasn't Jack. I gulped air as I pulled off my glove and grabbed the man's wrist. It was very, very cold with no pulse. I dropped it and sat up. The man was dead. An army pistol very like one Jack had brought back with him from the war lay on the ground a few feet away.

FOURTEEN

A s Lizzie and I waited inside the Dil Pickle, I thought
about what to say to Detective Whitbread. I would
tell him the whole truth. Never again would I mislead
my old friend. I'd done that before, and it only led to
heartbreak. I knew Jack couldn't have killed the man. But
Jack was already gone before the police came, and I had
no idea where he'd gone.

As soon as Whitbread came in from the police activity in
the alley, I gave him a faithful description of the evening.
Stiffening with apprehension, I even told him my son had
brought back a gun like the one I'd seen beside the body.

"Army issue Colt," Detective Whitbread said. He held up
a pistol with a long barrel. Cocking his hand, he swung out
the cylinder. "Two shots left." He showed us engraving on
the handle *U.S. Army Model*. "Most of the men returning
from the front brought back one of these." Whitbread
snapped the cylinder back in place. "We'll check it for
fingerprints but in this cold the shooter probably wore
gloves." He put the gun into a paper bag and handed it to a
uniformed man.

I told Whitbread that I had seen the dead man with Malcolm Murphy. "He introduced him as Frank Cervone." I had assumed he was a bodyguard. Had he been protecting Malcolm?

"Yes, he's known to us," Whitbread told me. The he put a hand on my shoulder. "You must be tired." It was well past midnight. "I'll have someone take you home." He looked me over. "Perhaps you could come to the office tomorrow and help me review the statements."

It was a huge concession, and I was grateful. "I'll be there," I told him as he led us out.

"Detective Whitbread, is it true the dead man was a debt collector?" The reporter had squeezed past the uniformed officer to approach Whitbread.

The detective rolled his eyes. "I've nothing to give you yet, Mr. Hecht. Just tell my man what you saw."

Hecht ignored him. "Did Jones owe him money? The IWW went into debt over the Bill Haywood trial. I heard Jones is having to sell part of the Pickle to get dough. Was Cervone shot for demanding payback?"

Whitbread shot out a hand to push the reporter back into the Dil Pickle. "Get in there, Hecht. Why don't you ask Jack Jones all about it?"

The reporter looked alarmed as he backed through the low doorway, closely followed by Whitbread and the uniformed man.

The detective provided a motorcar and driver to take Lizzie and me to Hyde Park. After he bundled us into the car, Lizzie slumped down in the sleep of the young, while I was left with my own thoughts. The Dil Pickle had been a wild, surprising environment in which to see my children.

But finding the body in the alley was more than surprising. It was dangerous.

I had assumed Cervone was a bodyguard, but now it seemed he was a debt collector. Whitbread hadn't denied the reporter's assumptions. Hecht had suggested Jones and IWW men might owe money. I knew people in the labor movement and, while they had my sympathy and support, I knew many of them were hard men. They would do whatever they thought they needed to do to destroy a system that oppressed them.

Hecht had claimed that the IWW men were in debt because of Haywood. Bill Haywood was the leader of the IWW. He and a hundred others were put on trial the previous April. They were accused of conspiring to hinder the draft, encourage desertion, and intimidate others and they were charged under a new espionage act. After five months that had included three straight days of testimony by Haywood himself, all the men were convicted. Haywood and a few others were sentenced to twenty years in jail. Huge amounts of money had been raised to fund the defense and provide bail. If Jack Jones had borrowed and not repaid the money, then a dispute between Big Mike's henchmen and the men of the IWW might have caused Cervone's death. I didn't think my children understood the forces at work in such a dispute, and I worried they could be caught in the crossfire.

I was exhausted and went to bed with the image of the dead man and the pistol lying in that alley in my mind, but I was so tired I slept anyhow. In the morning, Lizzie was gone before I rose. She left a note saying she was at the studio. I thought of talking to her about the Dil

Pickle shooting before meeting Whitbread but decided I
wanted to be prompt. Working with him would allow me
to uncover any threats to my children.

On the train ride, I thought about my long relationship
with Detective Whitbread. It might seem odd that
a university assistant professor should accompany a
police detective on an investigation, but Whitbread was
unorthodox in his approach to crime solving. From the
beginning of our association, when I'd first come to
Chicago so many years ago, he'd supported my research
and insisted that any useful understanding of the issues
required experience with the real problems.

For a time, I'd been at his right hand for every
investigation. He took on the task of educating me
in detection as part of my study of criminology. I'd
accompanied him to observe his investigations and he'd
come to rely on my note taking during interviews. We
grew apart when my brother was implicated in a crime.
Recently, we'd renewed the association between the
university and the police department, so once again
my students worked on police statistics. Now, however,
Whitbread was inviting me back into a partnership. I was
deeply grateful. I looked forward to playing that part again.

In his office at the Harrison Street station, Whitbread
reported what he'd learned. "Quite a few people left before
you found Frank Cervone's body," he said. "You say the
man came with Malcolm Murphy?"

"Yes. He and another man, Sean Riley. They followed
Malcolm around."

"Like bodyguards, you're thinking?"

"Yes. In fact, it reminded me of what you said about Big Mike having men to do his dirty work for him."

"That was about the death of Louis Graham. Those men may well be bodyguards for Malcolm. Do you think they're also involved in the Graham murder?" he asked.

"I don't. They just seemed to be at the younger Murphy's beck and call. But then I heard that reporter say Cervone was a debt collector."

"Yes. Cervone was a collector. He went after people who owed his bosses money. But he could have acted as a bodyguard as well. He knew how to rough people up. I'm not sure what he was doing at the Dil. It's full of Wobblies and anarchists like Jack Jones. Not Big Mike's kind of crowd."

"What about the reporter's suggestion that Jones might have owed money he couldn't repay? Malcolm Murphy claimed he had a partnership with Jones."

Whitbread grunted. "He wishes. More likely Big Mike wants to get rid of the competition. Probably thinks they draw drinkers from his saloons even though they don't serve alcohol. Mike's not a bohemian type."

Whitbread dismissed the suggestion that the IWW men shot Cervone. I suspected that Whitbread wanted to link the death of Cervone to the death of Louis Graham, the crime that City Hall had forbidden him to investigate. I wondered if he sympathized with the labor organizers. "You've been to the Dil Pickle?" I asked him.

"Incognito. They often get very distinguished speakers to show up."

I could picture Whitbread in one of his disguises, slumped on a bench like a hobo, enjoying the talk. He was unusually open minded and curious for a hardened policeman in his sixties. "Did you talk to Malcolm last night?" I asked him.

"He was gone. Jones wasn't sure when he left but Jones saw Cervone arguing with another man. Wouldn't admit he knew who the man was, though. Our first visit will be to the young Mr. Murphy. He lives with his mother in Bridgeport."

"That's the first Mrs. Murphy?"

"Yes. When Big Mike married again, he built the new wife a house out in Oak Park. His old house is in Bridgeport." He stood up. "I have a motorcar and driver waiting." His eyes glittered under shaggy brows. "You have a notebook and pencil?"

I pulled them out of my bag.

"All right then. To the hunt."

FIFTEEN

On the way, Whitbread told me about the first Mrs. Murphy. "She's quite a personality. They married young. Big Mike gave Eileen Murphy everything she could want, but he failed to pay her enough attention. She bore him a son, then she ran away to California with a musician." He shook his head. "When Mike's money ran out, the man abandoned her. Mike took her back. He built her the house in Bridgeport. To repent her earlier sins, Eileen became immersed in religion. She was so devout that she installed a priest in the private chapel at her house. Alas, the woman's nature won out and she ran away with the priest. Consumed by guilt, the man drank himself to death. Mike didn't take her back after that, but they say he's always supported her."

It seemed to me that Big Mike had questionable taste in women. One kept running off and the other was on trial for murdering a young lover. Did the man's twisted personal life have anything to do with the shooting death of Frank Cervone?

Malcolm and his mother lived in a gabled house set back from the street. A new motorcar stood in the semi-circular drive. We were led into a parlor by a maid.

As we waited, I looked around at the very visible signs of devotion. There was a gloomy oil painting of the Agony in the Garden and two separate crucifixes hung at each end of the room. The furniture was heavy black walnut with horsehair upholstery. Gold velvet drapes kept light out. Gas lamps fizzed over the fireplace. It wasn't a happy room.

"Detective Whitbread?" Malcolm wore an embroidered smoking jacket. I wondered if we had pulled him from his breakfast. "And it's Mrs. Chapman, isn't it? What can I do for you?"

"Have you heard that Frank Cervone was killed outside the Dil Pickle last night?" Whitbread asked.

Malcolm hesitated. "Yes. One of my father's men came this morning with the news. I was sorry to hear it."

"He was with you at the club last night?" Whitbread asked.

"Won't you sit down, Mrs. Chapman." Malcolm led me to a chair. I sat and took out my notebook. He frowned at that but motioned Whitbread to another seat. The detective declined and stood with his head cocked in impatience. Malcolm seated himself in a great chair that resembled a throne before answering.

"Frank came with me, yes. But he wandered away, and I didn't see him after the lectures began in the main room."

"Didn't you look for him?" Whitbread pursued his interrogation while I began recording.

"I assumed he had his own business to attend to. I believe there were a couple of people he wanted to approach to remind them of outstanding debts. If you know what I mean."

"Yes. I know he was a collector. Did he collect for you and your father?"

"No."

"Who did he want to see?"

"He didn't tell me specifically, but I did see him arguing at one point in the evening. It was with a friend of your son's, Mrs. Chapman. A Dr. Lieberman."

Eli Lieberman knew Frank Cervone?

"Did Dr. Lieberman owe money?" Whitbread asked.

"I wasn't in Frank's confidence about such matters, but I would assume so," Malcolm said. He reminded me of a cat licking his paws with satisfaction. He claimed not to know who else Cervone had talked to. He said he was with his other companion, Sean Riley, for the whole evening and offered the man's address if we wanted to check with him. Whitbread asked him when he'd left the club, and how he missed seeing Cervone's body in the alley.

"We left by a back door out to State Street. There is one, you know. As a future investor in the place, I know some of its secrets."

"Are you and your father trying to muscle in on the place?" Whitbread asked.

Malcolm looked offended. "Of course not, Detective. We're just looking for a business investment."

"You didn't take Riley and Cervone down there to try to intimidate Jones into letting you 'invest' then? Like you didn't take them to try to intimidate Louis Graham to stop seeing your stepmother, Flora Murphy?" Whitbread asked, poking a finger at him.

"I don't know what you're talking about." Malcolm was indignant. "If Frank Cervone went to see Louis Graham, it wouldn't be about Flora. I never tried to intimidate anyone. If you think a thug like Jack Jones would be intimidated, you're dreaming. More likely he had a private beef with Cervone. It wouldn't surprise me if Jones popped him." Malcolm frowned at Whitbread. His gaze turned to me. "And who says Frank Cervone had anything to do with Louis Graham's death? As a matter of fact, the day Graham was shot, I tried to prevent Jack Chapman from getting into a fight with him. Chapman was hot under the collar about Graham trying to court his sister while still seeing my stepmother. *I* tried to calm him down." He smiled grimly, knowing he had struck a blow at me.

Jack had argued with Louis Graham? I'd heard Jack was in the Monadnock Building and had talked to Malcolm the day Graham died, but this was the first I heard of a conflict with the dead man. Lizzie had mentioned going out with Jack, Agnes, and Agnes's brother but she hadn't seemed attached to the dead man. I kept my mouth shut. I was worried. My children were more and more deeply mired in the mud of these crimes. I knew the best solution was to get Whitbread to find the real culprits, but it was going to be messy. I dearly wanted to talk to Stephen about all of this.

Whitbread ignored the jibe about my son and went back to an earlier revelation. He was still digging into the murder of Graham. "Are you saying that Louis Graham owed money and Frank Cervone was trying to collect it?"

"We may never know, now that they're both dead, but money was missing from the Liberty Bond fund at our offices, and we believe Graham embezzled it. Since his death, the money losses have stopped."

"Why didn't you share this information when we investigated his death?" Whitbread narrowed his eyes.

"It's just another reason for Graham to kill himself, like my father says. My mother insists Flora killed Louis Graham, but that's natural since she hates my stepmother. What my father says is what happened. Graham killed himself over Flora."

I wondered about that. If Louis Graham stole his money as well as his wife, would Big Mike let it go? It seemed more likely to me that he'd have someone get rid of the problem. What if Frank Cervone had been involved and threatened to tell the truth about Graham's death? Could Malcolm and Sean have killed him?

Sixteen

B efore we left, Whitbread reminded Malcolm that Flora Murphy's trial would convene at the Monadnock Building on Monday. Despite the epidemic, the judge was moving the process along swiftly. He'd sworn in the jurors and completed the preliminaries. In the next step the entire court would visit the scene of the crime. Whitbread promised to take me there. Perhaps Fitz would come. The City Hall operative obviously took an interest in the fate of Flora Murphy. He wouldn't be happy to see the police detective at the trial, but it was a public event so Fitz couldn't very well exclude him.

Outside, Whitbread told the driver to take us to Cook County Hospital. He said he wanted to interview Dr. Lieberman about Cervone's death at the Dil Pickle. I wondered if he also planned to ask my son Jack about the day Louis Graham died. Even though Whitbread had been warned off the Graham murder, I knew he was determined to find the truth. The more I learned about my children's involvement with these people, the more uncomfortable I became. But I had to keep my trust in Whitbread and let the truth come out. I planned to look for Stephen after the interview to let him know what was going on. He was more clear-headed than I was when it came to Jack and Lizzie. I longed for him to reassure me that our children would come through this unscathed.

I led the way to the morgue, although I'm sure Whitbread had been there many times before. Repeating what I'd been told about the pandemic precautions, I warned him not to touch anything. As we hurried through the crowded corridors, I wondered if Dr. Lieberman would do the autopsy on Frank Cervone. He had probably done one on Louis Graham. Did Jack assist? How strange would it be to cut into the body of someone you had known? Was that even allowed? Seeing the overload of dead bodies stacked in corners when we arrived at the morgue, I thought they could not be too fussy about procedures when so many were dead.

I poked my head into the cold room. Jack and Eli were standing over three small bodies covered with sheets. The men looked pale and exhausted.

"More flu victims?" I asked. Whitbread stopped behind me in the doorway.

My son Jack looked at me blankly. Eli pulled out a stool and pushed Jack onto it. "Sorry, but we just had the most awful autopsy I've ever had to perform." He gulped for air and sat down himself, clutching at the tabletop. "It was a family. A wife and three children. He slit their throats—the husband. They were all down with the flu and he couldn't stand the suffering."

"He killed his own children?" I couldn't believe it.

"That's what this has come to," Eli said. His hand was shaking, and I saw him finger a silver flask in his pocket.

I stared at the shrouded little bodies. Under the sheets they would be cold and blue, when they should have been rosy and warm. I couldn't help remembering my own children when they were small. To have such young lives taken away like that was unimaginable. I shivered.

"It's driving men mad," Whitbread said with a great sigh. He looked away from the small bodies. "Last week a Spanish-American War veteran, delirious with fever, held off the police for two hours with a shotgun and two revolvers."

Jack looked up bleakly.

"It's despair," Whitbread said. "The sickness is barreling through their lives, and they see no way to stave it off. These desperate acts are their attempt to stop it. At another scene I attended, a woman set all the family's clothes afire inside the house. People are grappling with an invisible murderer."

The stories poured out of the police detective as if he'd been bottling them up till they burst. Police and doctors couldn't avoid the tragic scenes. They could only share the memories with others who'd seen the same kind of horrors.

Eli pulled out his flask and took a large gulp. Such madness surrounded us. It seemed useless to worry about one corpse shot in the chest when the piles of corpses were growing all the time.

SEVENTEEN

S ilent after the awful sight of the dead children, we followed Eli down to his office. Whitbread explained we were there about the shooting outside the Dil Pickle the night before. Did they know about that?

Jack nodded his head wearily, and Eli heaved his great shoulders. "The body's in there. We haven't gotten to it yet. If it wasn't brought in last night, we wouldn't have known. We both left the Dil before anyone found the body."

"Your mother discovered the body when she left the club," Whitbread said, looking for a reaction from my son.

"Oh, Mother, I'm so sorry," Jack said, looking appalled.

"I'm all right, Jack. You look like you're the one who's going to faint. Sit down."

Whitbread pressed on. "You were at the club last night, both of you?"

The young men mumbled "yes" while looking down at the floor.

"Dr. Lieberman, you were seen arguing with the dead man, Frank Cervone. What were you arguing about?" Whitbread asked.

Eli looked up. "Malcolm Murphy told you that, didn't he?" He walked over to his desk and took out his flask. Gulping a mouthful seemed to calm him. "It's true. When I saw Cervone come in with Malcolm, I tried to slip away, but he found me later. I owed money. Gambling. It's all such a gamble—life, on the battleground and even back here where we should be safe. I figure what's the point? If I win, I spend it in a night. Could be your last, always could be your last, you know." He took another sip then screwed the cap back on the flask. "It's no surprise my luck's not too good, eh?" He held up his artificial arm as if it were a symbol of his bad luck.

"Did you follow him outside and shoot him?" Whitbread asked.

"No. He followed me. He tried to grab me, but I hit him with this." He used his left hand to wave the artificial right arm. "Knocked him down and left. If he'd died of that, it'd be my fault, but no shooting was involved." He laughed. "I'm right-handed. Haven't aimed a gun since I lost it."

It sounded obvious when you looked at the rigid hand, but he managed to do autopsies single-handed. I wondered if Whitbread believed his claim about being unable to shoot a gun. The detective didn't question it.

Eli trundled back to his stool, hugging the flask to his stomach. Jack stared at him.

"What about you, Dr. Chapman. When did you leave the club and when did you last see Frank Cervone?"

Jack ran his hands through his dark hair. "I was with Miss Agnes Graham. I took her home. I didn't see Cervone after the main lecture began. I got my mother and sister seated then I went to look for Miss Graham. She wasn't feeling well, so I took her home."

"Without telling your mother where you were going?" Whitbread asked.

"Yes. I'm sorry, Mother." He looked distracted.

"Are you sure you didn't see Frank Cervone?" Whitbread pressed him. "Are you sure you didn't find Miss Graham in conversation with Cervone? Were you aware that Miss Graham's dead brother owed money for gambling debts?"

Jack looked like he was in a fog. "What? You think Louis owed money to Cervone's employers? No, never."

I couldn't keep still. "Jack, Malcolm Murphy accused Louis Graham of embezzling money from the Murphy company's Liberty Bond drive to pay gambling debts."

"That's absurd. Louis had his faults, but he didn't gamble. At least not enough to have debts. Malcolm's lying," Jack said.

"Was he lying when he said he tried to keep you from assaulting Louis Graham because he was courting your sister?" Whitbread asked. "Were you at the Monadnock Building to confront Graham on the day he was shot?"

I wanted to object. We were supposed to be investigating Cervone's death. Agnes and Jack were together at the Dil Pickle. Surely neither one of them had killed Cervone.

But Whitbread continued. "Did you perchance see Cervone at the Monadnock Building when you went to confront Graham the day of his death?" No one had mentioned seeing Cervone at Graham's office. Once again, Whitbread was trying to prove that Big Mike was behind the death of Louis Graham. "Did you tell Agnes Graham what you saw, and did she want to avenge her brother's

killing when she saw him? At the Dil Pickle last night, did
you help her get away or did you shoot the man for her?"

I wanted to groan, but I kept silent. Whitbread was
pushing my son, as I'd seen him push other suspects to get
them off guard and force them to admit secrets. What was
Jack hiding?

Jack turned red. "Leave Miss Graham out of this. She
had nothing to do with Cervone's death and neither did I.
We were both long gone. When we left through the alley,
Cervone was not there. I never saw Cervone the day Louis
died. I never saw Louis, only Malcolm Murphy. That's all."

Whitbread stared at him silently. I wanted to yell "Stop
it!" but I couldn't. I had promised myself I would let the
detective do his work without my interference. I couldn't
believe Jack had anything to do with either death. I had to
have faith that Whitbread would eventually prove my son's
innocence by finding the real killer. The silence became
painful.

Jack started sputtering, finally articulating, "Malcolm
Murphy is a sleazy liar. He told you about Eli's debts. He
told you I wanted to warn Graham off Lizzie. What he
didn't tell you was that I went to see him *before* looking for
Louis Graham to warn *Malcolm* about trying to seduce my
sister. I bet he didn't tell you that, did he?"

Eli stood up and threw an arm in front of Jack.
"Detective, I owed money and I did argue with Cervone,
but I didn't kill him. Jack left with Agnes Graham, but
they didn't kill him. Unless you plan to arrest one of us, I
think you should leave. In case you haven't noticed, there
are many cold dead patients out in that corridor waiting
for my knife. It's time we got back to them." He walked

briskly across the room to the door to the morgue and Jack followed him.

"Lieberman's right. I'm not ready to arrest anyone," Whitbread muttered. He looked at me as if assessing my reaction. I took a deep breath. "Don't worry, Emily. There's no evidence against your son, as yet. You might ask him about that pistol of his. If you can find it, I'm sure it would relieve your mind." He had purposely been provocative. I'd seen him do it to other suspects, but not my son. There was no truth beyond his bluster, I knew that, but still, it took my breath away.

He put his hat on, a bit uncomfortable with his performance, I think. He wanted to make it up to me. "You'll be joining me at the Flora Murphy trial on Monday, I believe. It will be at the Monadnock Building at ten. You could meet me at the office before then."

I agreed wearily. I told him I planned to find Stephen before leaving the hospital. He fastened his cloth mask and retreated out the door. I readied myself to talk to my husband.

EIGHTEEN

I found Stephen in his ward. He was helping an orderly move a sheet-covered body from a bed to a stretcher. A nurse waited with a wheelchair holding another patient. Stephen waved at me then helped settle the living patient before coming out. Taking my arm, he led me to a room that looked like an empty storeroom with no windows. There was a sink, shelves of supplies lining the walls, and a kitchen table with four chairs. A sofa and three beaten up old armchairs took up one corner.

A figure rose from the sofa, brushing sleep from his eyes. Stephen apologized, but the man waved him off, donned apron and mask then hurried out the door. As soon as it closed, I wanted to embrace Stephen, but he held his arms out to shoo me away. "There's too much chance of infection, Emily. We have to keep our distance." He pointed at the sofa for me and grabbed a chair by the table. Moving it to face me, he sat down, taking off his mask and cap.

I felt burned. Of course, he was right, but since Tommy's death I had come to rely on my husband's physical closeness to revive me when I was down. He was my compass to keep me on track when my emotions led me down dark side roads. I so much wanted to lay my head on his breast and hear his heart. Turning away, I plumped the cushions on the sofa.

"Stephen, I wish you would come home. I need your help."

"I know, but it's not possible until the infections slow down." In the harsh light of a bulb hanging from the ceiling, he looked pale, and I saw droplets of sweat. He got up and removed his outer layer, that great white swath of an apron. With that shroud stripped off, he looked more normal.

"Will it never end?" Beyond the concerns for our children and the mess I thought they were in, the flu was a great black inkblot on this page of history that threatened to obscure every other problem.

"There's no slowdown yet," he said. "Robertson will want to start opening businesses, but it's too early to remove precautions. I only hope we can keep him from letting down the guard. The man is such a political hack." Stephen was often at odds with the city authorities at the weekly meetings.

"You've never told me why you hate Dr. Robertson so much." It was unlike my husband to bitterly oppose anyone.

He rubbed his eyes. "Do you remember Dr. Theodore Sachs?"

"He was the head of the tuberculosis sanatorium, wasn't he?" I vaguely recalled there was a tragedy connected to his removal.

"He was the director when the mayor appointed Robertson to the Department of Health. Robertson kept trying to fill positions with other political appointees. The man is a quack. He doesn't believe in bathing. He even tried to push a fake cure and said the anti-bathing movement could eliminate tuberculosis. He hounded Sachs about financial matters, called him a dictator, finally forced him to resign after all the years Sachs had spent building up the sanatorium."

"Oh." Now I remembered. "Dr. Sachs committed suicide, didn't he?" I could see why Stephen was so bitter.

"Yes. Everyone knew it was because of Robertson, but he refused to step down. Did you know that now he wants to blame the flu epidemic on the Negroes who've come up from the South? The man is a charlatan."

"He is." No wonder my husband spurned Robertson. I wanted to support Stephen at the next meeting, but I remembered the trial. "Whitbread is going to take me to a hearing at the Monadnock Building on Monday. It's the Flora Murphy trial. She's accused of shooting a young man named Louis Graham." I poured out the whole story to him—the prison hospital scene where I'd seen Jack, the visit to the Dil Pickle and the shooting of Frank Cervone. I tried to explain how our own children were somehow tied up in these tragedies. He listened with his face in his hand, leaning on an elbow.

He sat up. "Emily, that's quite a story. But Jack and Lizzie aren't involved. You mustn't doubt that. You know they wouldn't hurt the Graham boy or this Cervone person." In my heart, I knew that, but I needed Stephen's confirmation of my belief. "Jack has been staying with Eli because of the fear of infecting you and Lizzie. I suggested he should do that," Stephen admitted. "As for Eli, I'm not surprised he has drinking and gambling problems. I suspect Jack is a steadying influence on him. He's had a bad time. Most of his staff were killed in the bombing that took his arm. His career is ruined, and he has nightmares. But he's a doctor. He's sworn to do no harm. I can't believe he would kill a man over debts."

"Perhaps not. But someone did." I wasn't as certain as Stephen was that Jack was helping Eli.

"Whitbread can find out who shot Cervone," Stephen said. "As for the hearing at the Monadnock, you may as well go. You're just an observer at the public health committee meetings. You'll probably do more good by assisting Whitbread. I wish I could help, but I can't leave now. We have to turn this thing around or an incredible number of people will die from this disease."

"I miss having you home."

He smiled. "I know. All the more reason for you to assist the police. It'll keep you from worrying. I'd like to meet this Agnes Graham who's gotten so much attention from Jack. But that introduction will have to wait."

Looking across at him, I thought of all those corpses piled up in the corridors, building a wall between me and my husband. I felt my heart in my throat. "If this disease is so dangerous, how can I leave you here? Haven't you done enough? Can't you come home with me now? What if you get sick? What would we do?"

He sighed. "Believe me, I'd love to crawl under a rock until this is over, Emily. But how can I? It's too late for that. This plague is sweeping over us and there's nothing to do but hold on and try to stay afloat. I won't go home until this is over. You and Lizzie shouldn't come here anymore. It's too dangerous now." He got up and came to me, brushing a lock of hair behind my ear. "It will be all right, Emily, I promise. We'll come through this."

I knew it wasn't in him to abandon the hospital. "What about Jack?" I wailed. Stephen knew I couldn't bear to lose another child.

He stepped back. "He'll do fine here, Emily. At the morgue they're not exposed to the disease nearly as much as on the floors. And I don't think you need to worry about Lizzie and these young men Jack wants to warn off. She turned down marriage a little more than a year ago. I don't believe she's ready to encourage suitors. The truth is, we're all just holding on waiting for this war and this epidemic to be over. Until then we have to just keep blindly pushing ahead." He walked to the door and held it open. "Emily, my love, go on home now, please. I promise I'll be back just as soon as it's safe. As for the pistol Jack brought back from France, it's in the bottom drawer of the desk in my study."

I took a deep breath. He was right and I knew it. I worried Jack might have shot a man, but Stephen had known immediately that the gun I thought I saw was safe in our home. He dispersed my fears like a breeze moving through clouds to let in the sun.

"Emily, I have to relieve one of the other doctors. We've had three nurses and one doctor come down with the influenza since Monday."

"Oh, Stephen." I knew he'd refuse to abandon his post. I was wasting his time, so I left, finding my way home by tram and railway.

Our Irish housekeeper, Delia, met me as I walked through our door. "Mrs. Chapman, you just missed Jack. He was here getting his clothes. He said to tell you not to worry but he needs to stay downtown. This flu is turning everything on end, isn't it? I've been helping my aunt and now she's come down with it. I'll have to stay to nurse her. I hope you don't mind. I just came to get more of my things."

Delia's aunt was Gracie Whitbread, the detective's wife. I hated to hear she was down with the flu. I helped Delia pack a bag and we shared a cold meal before she left. Before going upstairs for the night, I went to my husband's study. I had to check to be sure. When I opened the bottom drawer of his desk it was empty. Where was Jack's gun? Had Jack taken it? Just now, or in the past? Or had he come to check where it was and found it empty, as I had?

NINETEEN

I spent a restless Saturday night alone. If Stephen were home, he would have convinced me the absence of the gun meant nothing. Jack could have put it somewhere else. He never would have used it to kill a man. I knew that. But still I worried.

After talking to Stephen, I despaired of the effort to find the killers of Louis Graham and Frank Cervone. What were the deaths of two when hundreds were dying every week? There was nothing I could do to provide justice for the flu victims, but we needed to find and stop the human killers responsible for deaths that shouldn't have happened. I had no love for Frank Cervone, and I had never met Louis Graham, but they'd had their lives cut short, just as flu victims did. If they could be killed without consequences, then any of us could fall to the unknown killer. I knew at heart I was terrified I'd lose another child. I couldn't bear that.

Still worried about Jack's gun, I was loath to miss the opportunity to visit the scene of Graham's death. I wanted to understand what had happened to the brother of the young woman my son was seeing. And I wanted to understand what the dead man had meant to my daughter.

On Monday morning I met Whitbread at the station. I asked about Gracie, and he looked grim but said she was battling the infection at home with Delia's help. We walked to the Monadnock Building. One of the first skyscrapers, it was sixteen stories high with massive stone walls holding it up. Entering the building was like entering a fortified castle.

The trial was being convened in the building where the crime had happened. It was unusual, but not unknown for a judge to allow this kind of temporary venue in order to make the setting clear for the jury. I'd never been to a re-enactment like this before.

We took the elevator to Louis Graham's office on the fifth floor. In the outer office Whitbread stopped to finger the nameplate for 'C. Longman' on an empty desk. When he put it back, he raised an eyebrow at me as if to see if I understood the significance of the nameplate. I didn't. But I had seen him fixate on a detail like that before. While I had no idea what he was thinking, he would be leaping ahead, putting conjectures together to recognize a significant clue before I had an inkling of why it was important.

He murmured that he would see me after the hearing and shouldered his way through the crowd in the doorway. Although all were masked, I hesitated to follow. I feared infection.

It was a large room. The doorway faced a wall of arched windows. To the left, chairs had been set up in two rows for the serious looking men who were the jury. To the right, a big desk that must have been Louis Graham's was set up for the judge. A witness chair stood beside it and smaller tables were set out for the prosecution and defense. The lawyers didn't sit, however, they prowled like tigers in a cage near their tables. In the middle, two chairs and a couch looked like a stage set. There was a dark stain on the Oriental rug under the windows. This was where the young man had died.

I slipped in and joined a group of observers lining the walls. Whitbread had moved to a spot across the room near the windows. He turned and examined an opening where a staircase led up to the next floor. The internal steps up to the next floor was a feature in new office buildings to encourage a company to rent more space. If those were the stairs Malcolm had come down when he heard the shot, I assumed the Murphy family used the stairway to remain connected to Louis Graham's company.

There was a rustle of movement beside me as someone pushed through the crowd. "What's he doing here?" Fitz whispered in my ear. "He was taken off the case."

We should have known the City Hall man would be there. Whitbread risked getting into trouble by turning up. "It's such an unusual proceeding, he offered to take me." I tried to smooth things over as Fitz frowned at the detective who leaned against the far wall with his arms crossed.

"Come, I'll get you a seat."

Fitz took my arm and led me to a seat behind the defense table. On the other side of Fitz sat Big Mike Murphy, his large, knuckled hands grasping a cane in front of him. The judge entered, and the Sergeant at Arms called the room to order.

The prosecutor was a short man with a bald head and gold-rimmed eyeglasses. Flora Murphy's defense attorney was the famous Colonel Willis. According to the newspapers, he was a true charmer who could hold a jury spellbound with his stories. He spoke up to say that his client was indisposed but had requested that the trial begin. I suppose it must have been too much for Flora to return to the place where she'd watched her lover, Louis Graham, die, whether she shot him or not. What might she have revealed if forced to return?

The judge grudgingly pointed out it was the defendant's right to be present, but it wasn't required. He proceeded. In opening statements, the prosecutor promised to bring witnesses who would tell of a long-term liaison between the wife of the ward boss and the young neighbor. He also would show that Flora Murphy had purchased the gun that killed Louis Graham and that it was the extreme jealousy of the woman that led to the man's death.

When the prosecution finished, Colonel Willis spun a tale of blackmail and lust. According to him, the woman had been weak, falling into the arms of her young admirer. But then the young man demanded money. To get rid of him, she persuaded her husband to send him out West, but Louis Graham returned and once again tried to force himself on her, threatening to tell her husband of their former encounters. The defense lawyer claimed that Louis threatened Flora with the gun and the death was self-defense. Colonel Willis had abandoned the theory that Louis Graham shot himself and, instead, insisted the young lover was shot during a struggle over the gun.

What a nasty tale, whichever version was true. How could I have missed that Jack and Lizzie were involved with people who would stoop to such disgraceful behavior? In a world weighed down with war and epidemic, human passion could still wreak havoc. Had either of my children been infected by the passions in this squalid story? A crime of passion? I'd seen murders for money, for fear of exposure of a crime or reputation, even for revenge, but murder for love? Was that what this was all about? Right here in this room a tale of passion had played out. It was hard to imagine feelings turning so very bad as to end in a bloody death.

The first witness worked in a building across the street. He pointed out the window from which he had seen two people arguing. At that point, the prosecutor placed two men in the position as a demonstration. We could see how exposed the couple were in the large multi-paned window. The men had sheets of paper pinned to their backs identifying them as Mr. Louis Graham and Mrs. Flora Murphy. But they were middle-aged men with balding heads and mustaches. Strange stand-ins for the young couple.

The witness confirmed their placement. Colonel Willis could not get him to say he had seen a struggle, but he admitted he looked away before the shot was fired.

Next, the prosecutor called Malcolm Murphy to the witness stand. He glanced at his father nervously as he sat in the witness chair. When questioned, he pointed out the staircase he had come down after hearing the shot. The prosecution asked him to direct the two actors to show the jury what he found when he came down the stairs.

Malcolm posed "Louis Graham" on the floor, on his side, his legs drawn up. "Flora Murphy" he directed to collapse on the sofa. The prosecutor produced a small gun with a pearl handle. A tag attached with a string identified it as evidence. Malcolm placed it on the floor beside "Louis Graham." He frowned at his father as he returned to the witness seat.

He continued his testimony, saying that Flora had been hysterical, crying, "He's dead, he's dead." The prosecutor couldn't get Malcolm to say she'd admitted shooting Graham. I could see Murphy's son looked uneasy. He was walking a line between his own hatred of his stepmother and his father's desire that she be found innocent. Or was it because he knew someone else was there at his father's bidding? He avoided looking directly at his father who was staring at him. I glanced back at Whitbread. The detective leaned forward with narrowed eyes.

The prosecutor excused Malcolm with the comment that he would be called for further testimony when the trial returned to the courtroom.

Next, I was surprised to hear Dr. Lieberman called as a witness. Because of his current position at Cook County Hospital, he had done the autopsy on Louis Graham. The prosecutor had him explain that the bullet had entered the dead man's chest and angled downward to hit his spine. They displayed a chart and gave the jurors copies. The prosecutor asked if the wound could have been self-inflicted. He handed Eli the small gun.

"Not likely," Eli said. He took the little pistol and used his good left hand to angle it toward his chest. It was an unbelievable contortion. The prosecutor had proved Louis didn't kill himself.

Colonel Willis asked Eli to demonstrate the gun placement on the man impersonating Louis Graham who moved to the front of the room. Eli stood and pointed the gun at the man's chest, angling it down. Willis then told him the relative heights of Louis Graham and Flora Murphy and asked, "Wouldn't it be impossible for Mrs. Murphy to angle the gun down on the man like that since she is shorter than him?"

"Not impossible, but a bit awkward if he was standing," Eli admitted.

"Ah, but if they were struggling, perhaps rolling on the floor, then it would be possible, wouldn't it?" Willis had a gleam in his eye.

"There are many possibilities," Eli said. "They could've struggled, or he could've been sitting or kneeling. She could've been above him, or someone taller than Mrs. Murphy could've shot him. It is beyond my ability as a physician to say for sure what happened."

There was a hush in the room at the first mention of another, taller person. I glanced across at Whitbread. I could see him gritting his teeth to keep from commenting. I saw Fitz was also looking at Whitbread, then shaking his head. But Colonel Willis did not follow up on the suggestion.

The prosecutor jumped up and brought a chair with him that he placed in front of the witness. He grabbed the man who was impersonating Louis Graham and sat him in the chair, then turned to Eli who still held the gun. The prosecutor asked Eli to demonstrate how the gun would be held if the man was seated. The gun pointed down. The jury watched with interest but Eli raised an eyebrow skeptically as he was excused from the witness chair.

I thought the prosecutor was quick to skip over the suggestion that someone taller than Flora could have fired the shot. He seemed as eager at the defense to ignore the possibility of anyone else being present. I saw the defense attorney scribbling notes to himself. Usually, the elegant man was nonchalant but the back and forth about the shooting seemed to animate him.

When the judge adjourned the proceedings, Detective Whitbread quickly crossed the room. Fitz frowned. "Whitey, what're you doing here? You were warned off."

Whitbread grinned. "It's not Graham's murder I'm investigating. I have the Cervone case."

He'd purposely provoked Fitz who bristled. "That case has nothing to do with this. After all your time on the job, I'd hate to see you thrown off. I asked Mrs. Chapman to make you see reason, but you are very close to crossing a line you won't be able to come back from. This is your last warning." Fitz popped his hat on his head, tipped it to me, and left the emptying room. Whitbread frowned after him.

"Don't you think you should be careful?" I asked. I'd warned Fitz that Whitbread would do what he chose to do, and I couldn't stop him, but I worried my old mentor was close to being fired.

"Don't worry about City Hall," he said. "They've tried to get rid of me before." He took my arm and steered me out of the room and pointed to the nameplate on the desk in the reception area. "But where," he asked me quietly, "where, oh where is C. Longman?"

TWENTY

W hen I asked Whitbread what he thought of the proceedings, he was quick to point out that only Eli had suggested the possibility that another person could have been in the room. "Big Mike will be paying Willis's bill," Whitbread said. "I don't suppose he'd want that scenario in anyone's mind, even if it would help clear Flora."

Whitbread hung around the dead man's office, questioning men as they left the main room. He was unable to get any information about C. Longman from the police detectives and, when we were alone, he proposed asking Mrs. Flora Murphy in person. When I pointed out that he had no standing in the investigation and it was unlikely Mrs. Murphy would receive him, he shrugged. I sensed he was convinced that the missing C. Longman played some role in the tragedy. It was like him to refuse to explain until his suspicions were proved.

"In any case, Louis Graham's family lives close to the Murphy establishment and we can assume they will be able to tell us who this C. Longman is. There's a train leaving for Oak Park immediately. Will you come?"

Whitbread was being purposely provocative, but I was intrigued. How could I resist?

The ride was swift and the walk to the Murphy mansion on a shady street was quite pleasant. Whitbread insisted on knocking at the door. He would be in trouble if Murphy complained to City Hall, but he was in a rebellious mood. No surprisingly, we were met by a frigid manservant who insisted Mrs. Murphy was not at home. Undeterred, the detective led me to a small cottage down the street. "The home of the victim," he told me.

Agnes Graham answered the door. I was unprepared for the sudden meeting with my son's friend, and so was she. Her dark hair was pulled back, and she wore mourning. The atmosphere was so different from the Dil Pickle or the prison hospital where I'd seen her before. She was just as restrained in these home surroundings as my children were in Hyde Park. It made me think the young people must escape to the city to look and act as their true selves. I was coming to believe those true selves were unknown to me.

Whitbread introduced himself and asked for a few moments of her and her mother's time. I could tell Agnes was surprised to see me. She was struck dumb.

"Agnes, who is it?" A quarrelsome tone of voice rang out from within.

The young woman sighed and led us into a small parlor overly decorated with lace doilies and china figurines. She faltered as she introduced me as Jack's mother. Mrs. Graham, the distraught woman from the earlier scene in the prison hospital seemed only too anxious to talk to us. "That woman. She killed my baby. And now she's going to get away with it. Everybody knows that husband of hers has pull. He'll get her out of it. Oh, my poor boy. He was so young, so young and that woman..."

"Mother."

Mrs. Graham held a lace handkerchief to her mouth as if to stop it.

"You've been neighbors here for a long time?" Whitbread asked.

"Since before my husband died."

"And you knew the Murphys?"

"Not to speak to. Not at first. My Lou was only a schoolboy when we moved here. He used to help their gardener, to make pocket money. But she..."

"Mother, please. Anyhow, Mr. Murphy tried to help my brother." Agnes turned to us. "He set him up in that import business."

Mrs. Graham clutched her handkerchief to her heart. "My Lou was a very promising young man. Murphy knew that. He sent Lou out West to San Francisco last year on business. Lou did so well for him that when he came back, Murphy funded the business. Lou had great plans...if it hadn't been for her, that woman. I tried to..."

"Mother, please. Mrs. Murphy is on trial. She'll be punished. But that won't bring Lou back."

"Oh, I know, you're right. Nothing will bring him back. I don't know what we'll do now."

"We'll survive, Mother. We'll be fine."

"No mother can be fine when her only son's been killed."

"Yes, we are very sorry, Mrs. Graham," Whitbread said. "But there is one thing we were wondering about. When your son set up his office, did he employ anyone else? I noticed there was a desk outside his office and a nameplate for 'C. Longman.' Can you tell us who that was?"

The mother looked at her daughter then resumed sniffing into her handkerchief. Agnes replied for her. "That would be his secretary, Caroline Longman."

"I see. Can you tell me, was Miss Longman...it is Miss Longman, isn't it? Was she present when the tragedy happened?"

"I, I don't believe so." Agnes hesitated. "I haven't heard that she was."

"Was she usually at the office at that time?"

Mrs. Graham intervened. "We know very little about her. She was just a typist my son employed. We had nothing to do with her." She sniffed.

"Yes, I see. Do you perchance have her address or any contact information for the young woman?"

They looked at us blankly. But then Agnes said, "I believe my brother's address book is in the study." She left the room, returning with a piece of paper in her hand. "Here it is. I think it's somewhere on the north side."

Whitbread took the paper. "Yes. The north side. Thank you very much for giving us your time." He looked at a pocket watch. "If we hurry, I believe we can make the 6:15 train back to the city."

Whitbread appeared very grim as we sprinted for the train. On board, I asked what was worrying him.

"It is the absence of Miss Longman. I am very much afraid of what may have happened to Miss Longman."

"Surely the detectives who investigated the case must have looked for her."

"One would hope. But I fear for Miss Longman, I really do."

"You think she saw something?"

"Or heard something, or everything. If she was there that day, she must have."

"Do you think someone is preventing her from testifying about it?"

"We can only conjecture."

"You must find her." I was sure he would.

TWENTY-ONE

I was wrong. No one had seen the young woman since Louis Graham's death. Despite continued efforts, Whitbread could find no trace of her. I made a point of dropping in on my students working in the detective's office over the next few days to check on his progress. Whitbread was grumpy.

"There's no sign of the young woman, and I've been unable to question Murphy at all."

"Big Mike?" I asked.

"Yes." He drew me into the corridor where my students couldn't hear. "It's your friends at City Hall. They're protecting him. I've been forbidden to approach him at the saloon and out in Oak Park I get stonewalled by the servants. If anything happens to that young woman, you can blame it on Fitzgibbons and the mayor."

Whitbread had a low opinion of Fitz. In the past, they had managed to bury their differences at times of great danger, but they were like oil and water the rest of the time. In this matter, I had to agree with Whitbread. What if Murphy was responsible for Caroline Longman's disappearance? Surely the politicians wouldn't condone that. I didn't think Fitz would condone it, but it was no use defending him to Whitbread, the animosity ran too deep.

I gave an excuse and trotted over to city hall to find my old friend Fitz in his corner office. When I confronted him with Whitbread's accusations that City Hall was protecting Big Mike Murphy he grimaced as if he'd bitten into a lemon.

"It's only that Whitey is so rude. You know it's true."

I told Fitz about our theory that Caroline Longman might be in trouble.

He vehemently denied the possibility that Murphy might be responsible for her disappearance. "Nobody would defend Murphy if they thought he'd hurt a young woman like that. There's absolutely no reason to think he has done anything of the sort. Why would he?"

"That's what Whitbread wants to ask the man himself," I insisted.

Fitz shook his head. "Bothering Big Mike will cost Whitey his job, and he knows it. Oh, but let me see what I can do for you. Give me a minute, will you?" He got up and left me sitting opposite his large desk. Through the window I could see people walking along the street. I hoped he'd gone to get permission for Whitbread to interview Murphy although I doubted it. Nonetheless, I'd found over the years that it was better to challenge City Hall and to make them worry about a public backlash when they went too far, cooperating with powerful men. At Hull House we'd made a practice of pushing back at them.

Fitz came back wearing an overcoat. "All right, let's go talk to Big Mike if that's what you want."

Surprised, I followed him to a motorcar with a driver waiting outside. I could have objected and insisted he allow Whitbread to do the interview, but it was too late. And, besides, I wanted to meet this ward boss and make my own assessment of him.

We stopped at a busy side street in the Loop. Murphy's saloon had large glass windows sporting black- and gold-painted lettering. Copper doors opened and closed as men entered and left. It was lunchtime and working men would be getting a free lunch along with their beer or whiskey. My temperance minded friends condemned the practice, but it was common. Women weren't welcome in saloons, so I was uneasy, but Fitz led me to a door at the side where we were buzzed in and had to climb a steep set of stairs.

At the top, a couple of young men in shiny pinstriped suits jumped away from a card game. One of them opened the door on the left. From another room straight ahead, I could hear clicking noises, swear words, and masculine laughs. I assumed it was a gaming room. We were above the saloon.

Inside was a large room decorated with Oriental rugs and leather furniture. Behind a massive desk carved with lions on the front and paws for the legs, sat Big Mike Murphy, the man I had seen in the court hearing. His thick white hair was carefully coifed. His face was square and jowly, his eyes set deep inside a pit of wrinkles. He wore a dark blue suit with a polka dot tie and held a large cigar in the fingers of his right hand. He didn't rise when we entered. I could hear Fitz take a breath at that sign of disrespect, but Murphy simply glared at us from under dark eyebrows.

Fitz introduced me, and Murphy waved his cigar hand at a couple of chairs in front of the desk. His massive left hand covered a black telephone as if he were about to phone someone, the mayor perhaps, but when he heard my name, he removed his hand and pushed back from the desk, leaning back in his chair and squinting to look at me through the smoke. He took a considered puff on his cigar and tipped the ash into a large, hammered metal ashtray.

"Mike, we've come to consult you about a few things that have happened," Fitz said, clearly uncomfortable with our reception. "Mrs. Chapman was at the Dil Pickle the other night when a dead man was found at the door."

"A Mr. Frank Cervone, did you know him?" I asked. I really wanted to ask him whether he knew the whereabouts of Caroline Longman, but we had to start somewhere. I didn't want Murphy to confuse me with a polite Prairie Avenue matron. I had dealt with men of his type before, and I wanted him to know that I demanded truth from him.

When he didn't answer, Fitz swallowed and said, "Mrs. Chapman works closely with Detective Whitbread of the Harrison Street Station."

Whitbread's name was a charm. Fitz transmitted a subtle threat by using the detective's name. Murphy understood I'd come instead of having Whitbread pounding on his door. Murphy leaned forward with his elbows on the desk. "I heard about the shooting. That club of Jack Jones is full of IWW agitators. A bunch of troublemakers. I'm surprised Whitbread's not running *them* down."

"I understand from your son, Malcolm, that you have an interest in a partnership in the Dil Pickle," I said. I heard

Fitz inhale a breath at my boldness. But then he expelled and got talkative.

"Mike, what's this? You thinking of expanding into Towertown? I thought your establishments were all in the South Loop. That place doesn't even serve booze. The mayor will be interested in your plans, you know."

Murphy sat back. "That's all Malcolm's idea. He's deluded. The people up there don't have two cents to their name, but Malcolm insists they're all young and if you added booze, you'd draw even more people. He keeps telling me how many he sees there for the dancing on Saturday nights."

"They'd need a license," Fitz said, reminding Murphy of why City Hall was important to him.

Murphy grunted. "We'll see. Anyhow, if they're gonna have dead guys on their doorstep it's not the kind of place I'd be interested in. I heard about Cervone."

"You knew him?" Fitz jumped in. I could see he thought my attitude was making Murphy uncooperative and he wanted to mine the vein of sympathy he had with the man.

"Somewhat." Murphy looked at me. "Strictly speaking, he wasn't in my employ. He'd go after people to pay their debts if you know what I mean. If you have that kind of problem, you could employ him."

"And you did sometimes?" I asked.

"Not recently."

Cervone had come to the Dil Pickle with Murphy's son, but it occurred to me that Malcolm might have employed Cervone without telling his father, although I didn't know why.

"Do you have any idea who might have killed him?" I asked.

Murphy raised an eyebrow. "Someone he was shaking down for money? Maybe those IWW guys borrowed money for one of their labor actions and couldn't pay it back. Not my business."

"He was with your son," I told him. "You say you didn't employ him but, if so, why was he with your son Malcolm at the club that night?"

Murphy took another puff of his cigar, tapped the ash into the tray and sat back with his big arms folded. "Could be he was tracking down someone who might have owed money. Malcolm is in charge of finding out why funds are missing from our Liberty Bond drive." He fingered the cigar gently. "There was reason to believe someone took the cash to pay gambling debts. Cervone might have known who."

"Malcolm said it was Louis Graham," I said. "Did you think Louis Graham embezzled the money?" I heard Fitz move uncomfortably beside me and Murphy glared at me through a cloud of cigar smoke he exhaled.

"Yeah, it's possible Graham took the dough. He did the bookkeeping on it. I told Malcolm to find out." He tilted his massive head, considering me. I felt waves of tension from Fitz beside me. With his wife on trial, Louis Graham's death had to be a sensitive topic with the ward boss, but I wanted to raise it. I had to raise it to ask him about Caroline Longman.

"I was at your wife's trial of yesterday," I told him. "I was surprised she wasn't there."

"Mrs. Chapman—" Fitz began, but Murphy interrupted him with a wave of his big hand.

"That's right. I can't tell you why Flora wasn't there. It's a very painful subject. My wife and I have parted, at least during the trial," he said. He slumped in his chair. "She's not a well woman. She...Louis was a good boy. I tried to help him. I put up the money for the business. He was good at it." He looked across at me. There was a deep bleakness in him. I thought if I weren't a woman, he wouldn't have spoken like this. It was an appeal, I suppose, to my womanly sympathy.

"Mr. Murphy, do you know the whereabouts of Caroline Longman? We are worried for her safety."

He looked at me through the column of smoke. "Who?"

Did he really not recognize the name? "Caroline Longman. She was secretary to Louis Graham, and no one knows where she is."

He stared at me for a long moment, then, with a sigh, he sat up straighter in his chair. "No, I don't know the woman. The Graham boy had an unfortunate obsession with my wife. When she rejected him, he got a gun. It's only by luck that she survived." He told this off by rote, then shook his head as if waking up. "There's nothing more I can tell you."

Fitz stood and touched my arm. "Thanks, Mike. I knew you could clear things up for Mrs. Chapman. Emily, shall we go?"

I stood and let him lead me to the door. Looking back, I saw the broad shoulders of Big Mike Murphy collapse again. Had he ordered the death of Louis Graham, as Whitbread suspected? Had he arranged for Caroline Longman to be spirited away or worse? He didn't seem to recognize the woman's name. I felt uneasy. If he hadn't known of Miss Longman's existence before, he did now, because I had told him. Had I unwittingly put the young woman into even more danger?

TWENTY-TWO

When I returned to Whitbread's office, I told him about the meeting with Big Mike Murphy. "He claimed not to know anything about Caroline Longman."

Whitbread grunted. He was annoyed that Fitz had taken me to see the man while City Hall still refused to help him get an interview.

I bit my lip. "What if Murphy really didn't know about her? I hope I haven't caused that young woman trouble by mentioning her name."

"It's possible. We still haven't found her. I talked to a neighbor who said she moved here from a farm in Wisconsin. When we track down her family, I'll go up and talk to them. It's possible she went there."

"Mr. Murphy said he and his wife have separated."

"Because of the publicity." Whitbread pointed at a newspaper spread out on his desk.

I picked it up. The headlines were all about the war and how allied troops were finally driving the enemy back. Politicians discussed whether to negotiate peace or take the fighting into Germany. I fervently hoped they would stop the carnage. Below the fold in the paper there was a picture from the trial of Flora Murphy. It was from the previous week when they'd chosen the jury. The defendant sat at a table with a veil hanging from her hat while Colonel Willis stood asking questions of a potential juror. The story gave a lurid description of the scandal concerning the disgraced wife of Big Mike. I noticed a small block at the bottom about the rise in numbers of influenza deaths. The authorities were so anxious to minimize attention on the deadly disease it was disheartening.

I told Whitbread how Big Mike had claimed to barely know Cervone, the man I found shot to death outside the Dil Pickle. "He admitted his son, Malcolm, wanted to buy into the Dil Pickle but Big Mike dismissed it as a bad idea."

"Not Murphy's cup of tea. Too intellectual a group for him," Whitbread replied. "But Cervone could have been collecting for Murphy if Graham owed money. Cervone was the type of collector who took it out on a man's body if he couldn't produce the funds."

"Malcolm claims Louis Graham embezzled from the Liberty Bond drive. Could Big Mike have had him killed for that, instead of for being Flora's lover?" I asked.

"It defeats the goal of getting money back if you kill the guy," Whitbread pointed out. "But who's to say Cervone wasn't there trying to collect when Graham was killed? Maybe he saw too much. Or maybe he killed the man by mistake. Mistakes aren't tolerated in Big Mike's business."

"If he was there, maybe he saw Flora shoot Graham. Her lawyer is saying it's self-defense now. Perhaps Cervone knew it wasn't," I suggested.

"We'll never know what he saw now. But what did Miss Longman see?"

A thought rose, unwelcome, from the back of my mind. "Could she be dead, too?"

Whitbread shrugged.

I hadn't told Whitbread about how Jack's gun was missing. That bothered me. He could have taken it away after the shooting at the Dil Pickle or it could have been stolen. I wanted to ask my son directly where it was. But I had promised Stephen to stay away from the hospital and I didn't know how to contact Jack at Dr. Lieberman's place.

At supper that night I consulted Lizzie. I even told her about the gun.

"Jack would never shoot a man." Lizzie frowned. "I could see him lending the gun to someone else, though. You should ask him." She thought for a moment. "I don't know where Dr. Lieberman lives but I bet we could find them at the Dil Pickle tomorrow night. They're putting on a few plays and I've met Jack and Agnes there before to watch. They're short, modern plays that we particularly like."

I told her about my visit to Agnes's home with Detective Whitbread. "She was wearing mourning. I'm a little surprised she'd go to a place like the Dil Pickle so soon after her brother's funeral."

"Oh, Mother, what do you expect? Between the war and the flu, we could all be in perpetual mourning. The Pickle is an escape from all that. You can't show up in mourning."

I couldn't argue with her about that. We decided to attend the performances at the Dil Pickle the following evening.

The house was unnaturally quiet without the men. I marked papers in Stephen's study before retiring, but the room lacked its usual cheer without his presence. In bed, I felt cold even with extra blankets. I missed the warmth of his body beside me. I was tempted to visit the hospital the next day, but I knew he'd be annoyed with me if I did.

The next morning Lizzie retreated to her studio. I decided to attend the trial of Flora Murphy which was resuming at the Cook County Courthouse.

Twenty-Three

The Cook County Criminal Court Building was north of the river, at the corner of Hubbard and Dearborn. The large courtroom on the second floor was filling up. The judge, jury, and the witness chairs sat on a raised platform. Lawyers were separated from the rest of the room by a low railing. Wooden captain's chairs with rounded backs and armrests filled the room. At the far end, coats and hats hung from pegs on the wall.

There were only a few women present, mostly gathered at one side, but close to the front. I was lucky to get a seat among them. They wore swank hats and furs. I smelled heady perfumes. There was a tingle of excitement in the air. A trial of a woman for murder was unusual and they got vicarious thrills from it.

We were near the defense table where Flora Murphy sat wearing an old-fashioned black dress. A nurse hovered beside her. I saw her counsel, Colonel Willis, get her to remove her hat and veil. He wanted the jury to see her pale face and severely pinned blonde curls. She looked like a princess in a Pre-Raphaelite painting.

It was cold. Tall windows high up in the outside wall were opened as a flu precaution. We all stood for the judge, and he ordered the jury brought in as we sat down. Twelve men in dark suits took their seats in the jury box under the windows.

The prosecutor called Malcolm Murphy to the witness stand. I saw the young man glance at his father in the front row as he walked up. Malcolm looked worried.

The prosecutor briefly summarized Malcolm's testimony from the Monadnock Building, then asked him to describe a scene at a restaurant where Flora Murphy's jealousy over her young lover had been demonstrated. Malcolm looked at his father and swallowed, then told how Louis Graham had been at a table with his sister and another man and woman. Flora Murphy had accosted Louis calling him a cheater. "She accused the young woman of being a tramp and I had to pull her away to take her home to Oak Park," Malcolm said.

A wave of whispering rippled through the room and the judge knocked his gavel for silence. Big Mike was hunched over his cane and Fitz looked up in disbelief. The prosecutor approached Malcolm with a sly grin, waving a piece of paper. "Mr. Murphy, this is a letter to the dead man from Mrs. Flora Murphy, found in his desk. Please read the marked passage."

Malcolm frowned at the paper then read a few of the sentences Flora had written. "You always back your favorite horse, but you went on a fling and bet on a long shot. Now you must regret your bet, as the favorite always wins. You've put yourself on the level of the commonest racehorse tout by betting against the favorite."

It was a strange simile. She saw herself as the favorite and her rival as the long shot. At the defense table, Flora put her face in her slender hands. I shivered. Her words sounded demented to me, and I pitied the woman in the restaurant who'd been called a tramp because of Flora Murphy's vicious jealousy.

When Colonel Willis rose to cross-examine Malcolm Murphy, I saw the young man glance again at his father who was staring at him intently. The colonel asked about Louis Graham's gambling debts. Malcolm admitted that Louis had lost seven hundred dollars that Flora had given him by gambling.

"And is it also true that the dead man embezzled money from the company's Liberty Bond drive?" Colonel Willis asked.

"There was money missing from the fund," Malcolm said. "My father told me to find out where it went. But we've been unable to find the account books and I believe Louis Graham took the money to pay gambling debts."

Looking satisfied, Colonel Willis sat down. Malcolm looked relieved when he was allowed to step down.

The prosecutor called Agnes Graham to the stand. She told them that her mother was ill and unable to testify but that she could tell them about her brother's relationship to the defendant. The court specifically allowed Agnes to speak in her ailing mother's place. At that time, judges and juries always gave special leeway to women who were considered too physically and mentally weak for judicial procedures. It was an attitude that also worked in Flora Murphy's favor.

Answering the prosecutor's questions, Agnes described how Flora Murphy began calling out to Louis Graham when he was a sixteen-year-old boy on his way home from school. She would keep him for hours. Agnes told how when her mother went to talk to Flora Murphy, she went down on her knees to beg Flora to leave her son alone. It was terribly distressing testimony to give, and Agnes shook as she spoke.

Colonel Willis treated her with respect but managed to tell us that he would call a witness who was a servant in the Murphy household who would deny the statement that Mrs. Graham had gone on her knees to beg from Flora Murphy. He suggested the woman had exaggerated when she told her daughter of the visit.

I felt awful for Agnes Graham who had to sit through this polite assault on her mother's integrity. She shook with an anger she couldn't express as she stepped down.

The prosecutor called a witness to swear that Flora Murphy had purchased a pearl-handled revolver. Colonel Willis vigorously cross-examined the man and claimed he had witnesses to call who would swear the pistol was never received.

After that exchange, the judge adjourned for the day.

TWENTY-FOUR

I stayed in the city and met Lizzie's train from Hyde Park that evening. She carried a long burlap bag that flapped against her leg. When I asked what it held, she said, "You'll see."

I shrugged. If she wanted to be mysterious that was her choice. I wasn't too curious. I was preoccupied with thoughts about the trial I'd attended. I was deeply disturbed by the descriptions of the illicit love affair and the vicious emotions of jealousy. I wished my children would distance themselves from the sordid tale of love and murder, but I hesitated to be blunt with them about my concerns. I despaired of a way to make them realize the danger to themselves in the situation. I still felt uneasy about the missing gun Jack had brought back from France. And I wanted to ask discreetly whether he had, in fact, warned Louis Graham against courting Lizzie.

When we reached the alley with the green light over the small orange door, I shivered. I had spent several cold hours there the night I found the body. The word "Danger" painted above the door was ominous, despite the more lighthearted phrase: "Step high, stoop low, leave your dignity outside."

We stooped over the threshold, avoided the grim reaper who was still accosting potential carriers of the flu, and found Jack and Eli chomping on sandwiches in the outer room. Both had shadows under their eyes and cheekbones. I suppressed a motherly urge to scold them about getting enough sleep. My children had allowed me to slip through the barriers into their world and I was aware that it was an unusual privilege for a parent. So, I swallowed my advice.

Jack left to get us coffees and Lizzie slipped onto a stool beside Eli. He looked bleary eyed, and his silver flask stood beside his cup. He was hunched over a plate, eating his sandwich as if he were starving. To get his attention, Lizzie rudely tapped him on the shoulder. "I've got something for you," she said.

At that, he sat up and wiped his mouth with a pocket handkerchief, squinting at her.

Lizzie bent her head to extract something from her burlap bag and dropped it on the table in front of him. It was a man's leg.

Eli choked on his last bite. Lizzie whacked him on his back, and he coughed. "That's better," she said. "Have a sip of your coffee." When his hand crept toward the silver flask, she grabbed it and moved it away. "So, what do you think?" she asked, grasping the leg by the foot. "Didn't I tell you you could do better? See the articulation of the ankle? Isn't that worlds better than what you have now?" She held the foot up to his eyes. "The foot itself needs to be the right shape to wear a proper shoe, you see?" Lizzie's eyes glowed with admiration for her own work.

"Good lord, what is that?" Jack asked as he placed coffee cups in front of me and Lizzie.

"A leg, of course, are you blind?" Lizzie said.

Eli reached out and took the leg by the calf. Turning away he balanced it on his artificial right hand while examining it with his left. "It's light," he said, bouncing it up and down.

"It can be heavier if that's what you need," Lizzie protested.

"No, no, it's better this way."

Lizzie turned happily to her coffee. "I told you so."

"Right, can we get that off the table?" Jack asked.

Eli ignored him, turning to Lizzie. "We could use two dozen more. I've got a waiting list."

Lizzie's mouth opened with outrage, but at that moment Sherwood Anderson joined us. As Lizzie stuffed the leg back into her bag, Anderson slapped a flier on the table. It announced the three one-act plays to be performed.

Anderson greeted me and took a seat. "You'll enjoy this," he promised. "Jones and his hoboes do the scenery, and they get regulars to take the parts. They did Ibsen's *Hedda Gabler* with one of our ladies of the night in the starring role last week. She was pretty good. Hi, Ben!"

Ben Reitman was the physician who advocated contraception that my children had listened to in Bug House Square before my previous visit to the Dil Pickle. In his flowing cape and broad-brimmed hat, he wrapped an arm around Eli. "Evening," he said. "I'm just going to take this man away for a little confab—Eli." He led Jack's friend away.

"Eli helps him with the clinic," Jack said. Lizzie nudged him and he looked at me and blushed. "Sorry, Mother. I don't know if you're aware of Reitman's work."

"Oh, yes," I said.

Jack looked relieved not to have to explain and he promptly changed the subject, encouraging Anderson to talk about other plays he'd seen at the Dil Pickle. I got the impression that Jack was afraid I was priggish enough to be embarrassed by the fact that Reitman's clinic treated venereal disease and offered contraception. Young people have such a skewed picture of the older generation, especially their own parents. I was tempted to tell my children a tale of how their father had worked part time in brothels when he was first in Chicago. The doctor who attended prostitutes was known as "the professor" in such establishments. Stephen was sorely embarrassed when a young student recognized him and addressed him as such in my presence. But my past and Stephen's past were so far back in antiquity to my children that such a thing was inconceivable to them.

I kept my mouth shut with an effort. It was Stephen's story to tell. I could picture him at the Dil Pickle with us after this terrible influenza was over. I'd be surprised if he didn't tell the story himself. Imagine the surprise on Jack and Lizzie's faces. Young people are easily shocked.

I didn't have time to talk to Jack alone before we all moved to the room where a stage was set up with painted backdrops. I'd have to wait for the plays to finish to ask him about the missing gun.

The first play took place during a labor strike with two women waiting in vain for a husband and father to return. The second play opened in an attic shared by two cocaine addicts, a man and a woman, and the man was Dr. Lieberman. My mouth dropped, but the others weren't surprised. It was a sad story ending with a suicide pact as the two forlorn souls turned on the gas and lay down to die. Luckily, they didn't have a coin for more gas when it ran out. I was glad to see them raise the window shades and choose life. The third play was about an Irish revolutionary who perished of course.

During the applause I managed to lead Jack out of the room to ask him about the gun.

"After Cervone was shot, I thought Eli and I might need it for protection." He ran a finger around his collar. "We heard he was killed after I left to take Agnes home. Eli told me about it." I should have been relieved but something in his story didn't ring true. He looked at me. "Mother, you can't think I killed that man."

"No, no. It's just that when I saw that gun lying there beside him, it looked like your pistol."

"It wasn't mine, I promise you. Besides, I didn't know Cervone. I mean he came looking for Eli once, but that's all. I told Detective Whitbread that."

I reached out a hand to his shoulder. He seemed upset. "Of course, I know you didn't use your gun to shoot Frank Cervone, Jack. But I wonder about your friend Eli."

"Mother, Eli saw a lot of disturbing things in the war. And he lost so much. He's having a hard time. But he's a doctor. You can't believe he would hurt anyone. We've sworn not to. Both of us."

"In that case, please be careful how you use that gun," I said.

Jack shrugged and turned back to the rest of our party before I could ask him about warning off Louis Graham. While he returned to Lizzie, a figure stretched out in a chair leaning back against a wall caught my eye. The dilapidated hobo looked familiar. He was gaunt, long legged, and dirty with long hair under a floppy felt hat. A thin salt and pepper beard straggled down his chest. He wasn't looking at me, but toward Jack. I followed his gaze to Jack's friend Eli. I blinked. Yes, I recognized that intense gaze of the otherwise sloppy hobo. Of course. I'd seen him in disguise many times over the years. It was Detective Whitbread.

TWENTY-FIVE

J ack and his friends were in conversation with Eli about his part in the play. Since they paid no attention to me, I was able to saunter over to the detective. "What brings you to the Dil Pickle?" I asked.

Under the brim of his hat, Whitbread's cool eyes wandered over the sparse crowd in the room. "Looking for more information on Mr. Cervone. The Wobblies who run the place are a lot more talkative to a hobo than to a policeman."

I noticed several men nod at Whitbread and one yelled, "Hey, Paulie."

"It's not the first time you've been here as a hobo, is it?" I asked.

He took out a pipe and began to dig out tobacco from a dirty pouch. Like most of the men in the room, he had removed his mask and stuck it in a pocket. "It's useful to keep track of what's going on."

"Did you find out anything about Cervone's murder?"

"I talked to Jones in my present persona while we set up the scenery this afternoon." Whitbread nodded at the men across the way. "Jones was a little cagey. He claims he's getting a lot of pressure from Murphy's son to sell part ownership. But there's something else going on. They're up to something. We know Jones was visible in the club the whole time, so he couldn't have done the shooting, but he did say there were others who weren't happy about Murphy trying to extend his influence up here in Towertown. With the number of anarchists and revolutionaries around here, one of them could have decided to knock off a Murphy henchman as a warning to stay away. Jones claims ignorance, but I think he knows something." He puffed on his pipe to get it going after lighting it with a match. The earthy smell was more pleasant than the tang of cigarette smoke that also hung in the air. "There's something fishy about this deal with Malcolm Murphy. I don't believe it's about selling this club.

"It's hard to believe no one saw anything," Whitbread continued. "Jones hinted that Cervone confronted someone before he left. I'm pretty sure it's Dr. Lieberman. Lieberman's very friendly with the more radical elements in the crowd up here. If he got someone to get Cervone off his back, they're too chummy a group to admit it. I didn't tell Jones that Lieberman had already admitted to an argument with Cervone."

I looked over to where Eli was hanging onto Jack's shoulder. Malcolm Murphy sidled over to Lizzie's side. It seemed to me that Whitbread was no closer to finding the shooter. I saw Agnes Graham enter the room. She frowned when she saw the group with Jack and Lizzie. She put her head down and marched toward them.

"I'd better go back to my children," I said.

Whitbread also saw Agnes. He turned his back toward her and the table of Jack's friends, leaning toward my ear. "I'll be going out of town tomorrow to Wisconsin, to see if Miss Longman is with her family or if they know where she is. In case I'm not back in time, you might want to attend the trial. If they finish calling witnesses, they'll be having the final statements. When they send the Flora Murphy case to the jury, I'd like to have a first-hand account of what they say."

"Yes, of course. Good luck in Wisconsin." I was disturbed by what I had heard at the trial. I wanted to hear out the rest of it. I knew my children's friend Agnes must be very hurt by what was being said about her dead brother. I only hoped Jack and Lizzie would stay out of the courtroom. An attempt to support their friend could complicate their lives without helping her. I went back to the table, arriving just as Agnes stood in front of Jack.

"So, this is where you are," she said to him.

"Of course, I thought you wanted to see the plays like we usually do." Jack took a step backwards.

Agnes shook her head and looked cross. She nodded to me and Lizzie but pursed her lips when she saw Malcolm Murphy. "Malcolm, you have a nerve showing up here. How dare you blame Louis for the stolen Liberty Bond money? You know he was honest. He'd never steal from your father." She glared at him.

Malcolm straightened up and looked embarrassed. "I'm sorry, Agnes. When the police asked me, I had to tell them the truth. More than ten thousand dollars disappeared, and your brother kept the account book that's been missing ever since his suicide."

The young woman's mouth dropped open. "Suicide? Louis didn't kill himself. Your stepmother shot him." Her face was so pale, I thought she might faint. Jack saw it, too, and moved to her side. "What makes you think the account book would show any wrongdoing on my brother's part? Maybe you're the one who has a lot to *account* for."

Rather than inflame her anger, Malcolm chose to retreat. "I can see you're upset. I'll say goodnight." He turned his back and moved away. I was surprised that he was wise enough to let her fire burn out instead of fanning the flames by arguing with her. But when Jack attempted to put a supportive arm around her shoulders, Agnes shook him off.

"What are you doing with him?" She pointed at Eli. Her breast rose and fell with quick breaths, she was so agitated. "You know he tried to get Louis involved in his gambling schemes."

Jack sighed. They must have had this argument before. "Agnes, you're mourning your brother, but you know as well as I do that Louis was no angel." They stood still, facing each other. I thought Jack was cruel. It was natural for her to defend her recently dead brother from accusations of embezzlement and gambling debts.

Lizzie appeared to be holding her breath beside me, while Eli took a chug from his silver flask. When he put it down, Jack shook himself, grabbed the flask and took a large gulp. Agnes's face reddened and she reached out to the table to support herself before pushing off from it and heading to the doorway.

Jack hugged the flask to himself as he watched her walk away.

"Oh, Jack," Lizzie murmured.

Eli grabbed the flask back from Jack. He waved it at us. "I just want to say, I never tried to corrupt the angelic Louis. If he found his way to a dice game, it wasn't me that led him."

Lizzie touched my arm. "Mother, I think it's time for us to go."

TWENTY-SIX

When we reached the orange door, Malcolm Murphy was waiting with his man beside him.

"Can I offer you ladies a ride home?" he asked. "I have my motorcar at the back door. It's a cold night, too cold for you to be walking around."

I wasn't looking forward to the cold night air, but I didn't think Lizzie wanted to accept Malcolm's offer. She said, "Thank you, Malcolm, but we'll be all right." She looked at me. "My mother's always telling us how she has spent years traipsing around the city at night."

Malcolm wore an overcoat with velvet lapels and a shiny silk tie. He held a tweed cap in his hands in front of his chest. "Please. I insist. I want to show off my new Packard. Sean and I will sit up front and there's plenty of room for you ladies in the back." When Lizzie hesitated, he said, "You don't want your mother sitting in the cold with the influenza around, do you?"

With a glance at me to confirm I wanted to accept, Lizzie gave in, and Malcolm led us through the coffee shop to a doorway on the other side of the building. "This is the back way," he bragged. He was proud to show off his inside knowledge of the place, but he wasn't overbearing. In Lizzie's presence, he seemed to soften his attitudes more than I'd ever seen before. But no matter how smitten he might be, I could tell that Lizzie was content to fend off his advances. I believed it was for my sake alone that she'd relented and accepted his offer.

Through a small kitchen and then a long dark tunnel we reached an open area on State Street. The motor car was two toned with a gleaming black nose and roof, a tan body, and white walled tires on chrome rims. Malcolm bundled us into the spacious back section, cushioned in soft tan leather. There was room for four people, but he shut the door and climbed into the driving seat in the separate front cab. His henchman climbed in beside him after cranking the engine. The motor was powerful and quiet. The ride was smooth. Lizzie and I leaned back in the luxury of the car which brought back memories of my dead son who had been so enamored of motor cars before his death.

"Tommy would have loved this," Lizzie said, echoing my thoughts.

We rode in silence, only speaking to the men to give final directions to our townhouse. Malcolm helped us out of the car and up the steps, but he declined to come in. I was grateful because I was exhausted. Lizzie didn't even thank Malcolm for the ride. I did. I worried about the company my children kept. Agnes and her poor brother were embroiled in the Flora Murphy scandal. She accused Eli of gambling and he obviously had a problem with drink. Malcolm had a notorious father, but I appreciated that he had cared enough to see us home. I hoped Jack and

Lizzie would be able to extract themselves from that circle of companions. Perhaps Stephen could convince them. I knew they would only resent any criticism from me.

Inside, Lizzie suggested we warm up with a fire in the study before retiring and I agreed. In Stephen's study, she quickly set up a fire, lit it and sat on the floor feeding kindle as it got bigger and warmer until she added a couple of split logs and sat back.

"Malcolm was over in France, you know," she said.

"I didn't know that."

"He wasn't in the trenches. He was a supply clerk or something." I immediately assumed his powerful father had set him up to oversee a black market, then I silently scolded myself when she said, "His warehouse was bombed. He was burned but he helped get one of his fellow soldiers out. His father was able to get him brought back to Chicago and discharged after that."

"He seems fond of you."

Lizzie shifted and added more kindling. "He's a little too attentive sometimes, but I try not to be rude."

I watched her closely. Since her failed engagement at the start of the war, Lizzie had seemed to avoid social engagements, instead devoting herself to her sculpting. It worried me sometimes, but Stephen thought it was healthy. Now that I knew that my children inhabited a world with very different social activities, I wasn't sure what to think. But as Stephen had claimed, she appeared to be guarding her feelings, unwilling to indulge them. If she began to drop her defenses, I hoped it wouldn't be for the questionable Dr. Lieberman.

"Apparently Jack warned off both Malcolm and Louis Graham," I said. "Did you know he objected to their attentions toward you?"

"Jack as the big brother." Lizzie shook her head. "When I heard that he spoke to Malcolm Murphy, I told Jack to mind his own business."

Lizzie resented efforts to protect her, but I could understand Jack's concern. Her engagement had ended badly after so much anticipation of a big society wedding. It was hard to know if she ever regretted her decision to withdraw from all that. I wondered about Louis Graham, too. Was she grieving his death? "Lizzie, what about Louis Graham? Were you close to him?"

"Louis was really very sweet. And a bit naïve. Truth is, Mother, I used Louis to keep Malcolm off. I wasn't really attached to him at all. We were friends. He was having a difficult time." She looked up at me as if assessing how much to tell me. "I think he felt trapped by his feelings for Mrs. Murphy. He was a lot younger than her you know. He met her when he was still a schoolboy and he used to cut her lawn. I think he fell in love with her, but he felt it was wrong all the time. He felt desperate sometimes, I think. I provided a kind of cover for him, with his sister and his mother. Just as he provided a kind of cover for me with Malcolm and Jack and anyone else who wanted to get too close. When Jack found out about his connection to Mrs. Murphy, he got all upset. I think Agnes told him. Jack didn't realize that I already knew all about Louis and Flora Murphy."

"Jack seems very fond of Agnes," I said.

She looked down. "Yes, and that scene tonight was awful. Agnes was so angry at him."

"She seems to think Dr. Lieberman's a bad influence. I didn't like the way Jack responded to her. I can see why she stormed out," I said.

"But it's bad for Jack. Bad for both of them." Lizzie looked up at me earnestly. "They are very much in love, Mother. I feel like I have to do something to make peace between them. I'll talk to Agnes."

I felt stung. Jack was in love with Agnes Graham. Lizzie would know. But Stephen and I were in the dark. Perhaps Stephen knew more than he ever told me. How long had they been seeing each other? I knew so little about her. My children's generation had thrown off all the old traditions of proper introductions and chaperones. I could sympathize with the need to reject tedious rules of society. But those old broken conventions had served to keep young people safe. Too safe for a group that insisted on their freedom. When I was young, I had chaffed at the strictures of society but from the perspective of a parent I could see they were trying to keep the young and naïve safe. I'd never tried to hide the bad things in the world from my children. I had to trust that they would be able to handle their brushes with evil in the real world.

"You don't think your brother will resent your interference?" I asked.

"I feel like he was suspicious of Louis for my sake and that's caused the rift with Agnes. So, it's at least partly my fault. I must do something to make it right between them. I know where she works at the Art Institute. She'll be at the trial tomorrow, but I know she'll be hard at work Saturday.

I'll talk to her then. The longer they're apart like this, the harder it will be for them to heal. Agnes loved her brother and she's missing him. She can't lose Jack, too."

"Perhaps I could go with you?" I wanted to meet Agnes Graham somewhere that I could get to know her. If my son loved her, I needed to understand why he was so attracted to her. Stephen would have told me it was Jack's business, and I should trust him, but I couldn't be sure without getting to know her myself. My mind was rushing to remember every time I'd met her, and it was unsatisfactory. I bit my lip.

Lizzie looked up at me. She saw my concern. "Yes, of course. You should get to know Agnes better. You'll like her, I promise."

I hoped she was right. Meanwhile, I was drawn to the trial of Flora Murphy. I, too, would attend the next day.

TWENTY-SEVEN

I arrived early and found a seat near the back of the courtroom. The murmurs and rustling of the crowd stopped when the judge and jury entered.

As a final witness the prosecutor called a salesman from a gun store who produced a bill for a pistol similar to the one used in the crime. It was signed by Flora Murphy. The defense attorney got the man to admit the bill had never been paid although their records said it had been delivered to the Murphy home.

The prosecutor rested his case and Flora's attorney began calling witnesses.

First Colonel Willis called the housekeeper from the Murphy's house. After establishing that she had worked for Big Mike over twenty years, he asked about the visit Agnes Graham had described when the dead man's mother had begged Flora to leave her son alone. With a look of haughty disapproval, the housekeeper denied that Mrs. Graham had ever gotten down on her knees.

I could see Agnes's back straighten and I thought she must be quivering with indignation at this implied accusation that she had lied. The prosecutor attempted to shake the woman's testimony, but she stood firm.

Next the defense called an elderly woman named Mrs. Brady. She was stooped and had a wrinkled face, calloused hands and a sly look. Prompted by Colonel Willis she claimed to have overheard a conversation between Flora Murphy and Louis Graham. She said the dead man had threatened the defendant, demanding she get money from "the old man." I looked around. Big Mike was not in the courtroom, but I saw Malcolm Murphy sitting behind the prosecution. His shoulders were hunched. He must be angry. Mrs. Brady even claimed that Louis had begun to strangle Flora. At the end of her statements, she cackled, and Colonel Willis quickly sat down.

I saw the prosecutor bang a paper on his desk at this statement. Red in the face, he collected himself and stood up to face the old woman.

"Mrs. Brady, are you aware of the fact that it is a crime to lie to us in this courtroom where you have taken an oath to tell the truth? That is called perjury and can result in a prison sentence."

Colonel Willis objected but the judge waved him away and Mrs. Brady cackled. "I wouldn't lie, not me," she said, smiling at the prosecutor.

Under questioning she claimed she was hidden behind a billboard outside a restaurant and had overheard the argument. When he questioned why such a conversation would be held in public, she shrugged. When challenged on how she could see an attempt to strangle Flora Murphy if she was hidden behind a sign, she claimed she stepped out and her appearance was the only thing that had stopped the assault. When asked about receiving money from Big Mike, she shrugged and reluctantly revealed that she worked for him in one of his saloons. The prosecutor warned of actions against anyone who lied at the trial, but the judge admonished him to take that argument to another court.

Next, Colonel Willis examined Flora's maid who claimed that no revolver had ever been delivered to the Murphy household. After much elaboration on that topic, Colonel Willis asked about the night before the shooting. The maid said she overheard an argument between Flora and Big Mike. She only heard words like "blackmail" and "papers," but Colonel Willis managed to suggest that Flora had confessed to her husband that Louis Graham had been blackmailing her for years and Big Mike had told her to stop paying him and get back her letters once and for all. Despite many objections from the prosecutor, and his cross-examination that revealed the maid was listening behind a thick oak door, the defense managed to plant the picture of the argument.

Finally, the defense brought two witnesses from the Monadnock Building who claimed Flora had yelled, "He killed himself, help him," and that she had not been holding a gun in her hand.

The judge adjourned the trial for the weekend and said he expected final arguments on Monday. I was depressed and exhausted as I found my way back to Hyde Park that evening.

I knew the lawyers would twist and color the facts in a courtroom, but I was distressed with what I had heard. My children admitted they knew both Louis and Agnes

Graham, in fact they were close friends, closer than I'd imagined. Even though I knew it was a distortion, the dead man's obsession and the accused woman's wild jealousy were ugly to contemplate. Even worse was the notion that Louis Graham had been a blackmailer and thief. I doubted the story the defense was pushing, trying to tarnish the memory of the dead man, but, even so, the thought that he might have courted Lizzie worried me. I believed he was only a friend and a sort of defense against other suitors. She believed that. But she couldn't escape the sordidness of the story. I was relieved that, at least, her name had never been mentioned in court. I tried to take some solace in that.

TWENTY-EIGHT

The next morning, Lizzie and I looked for Agnes at the Art Institute. The gray stone building looked like a temple with a triangular pediment and tall archways. We climbed the steps between the two proud stone lions standing guard. Inside, Lizzie merely nodded at a ticket taker behind a counter that stood before the grand staircase in the lofty atrium. A group of school children followed a guide up the steps. On a Saturday, the place was empty.

If I was awed, Lizzie certainly wasn't. She took a quick turn to the left and I followed her down plebeian stairs to the basement. She took me along a hallway where the echo of our footsteps on the tiled floor was the only sound. Broad oak doors on both sides were closed or open to darkened studios. A string of lights along the ceiling lit our way.

"Most of us don't come in on Saturdays, but Agnes likes to work on her own things, not class assignments, so I know she'll be here," Lizzie told me.

An abrupt noise ripped through the air, a shot that echoed against the stone walls.

I halted, grabbing Lizzie's arm. "What was that?"

But she pulled away from me yelling, "Agnes! Agnes!"

She ran down the hallway, and I followed. Light spilled from a doorway, and we rushed inside and saw a heap on the floor. I heard a door slam in the corridor. Bright red blood pooled under Agnes's body. Lizzie gently pulled up her shoulder to see her face. I saw the girl's eyes roll and she groaned.

"No, let her lie flat, get something to stop the bleeding," I said. "Something clean." She was curled up, clutching her stomach. I thought she had been hit in her abdomen and blood was spilling out to the floor. A palette patterned with blotches of colored oils had fallen to the floor, and a table with brushes and tubes of paint had overturned.

"Here." Lizzie found a clean apron in the satchel she carried and handed it to me. We gently turned Agnes over and I pressed the cloth against her middle. She had gone slack in a faint. I sent Lizzie for help. Gulping back a sob, she hurried away.

I murmured that help was coming as I held the cloth to stem the blood. A wisp of smoke still hung in the air from the gunshot. The smell turned my stomach. An easel with a painting had smashed to the ground in front of Agnes when she fell. It was a blur of dark colors. I looked around. The room was obviously shared, each student owning a corner where they had piled canvases and supplies with charcoal and pencil drawings taped to the walls.

Whoever had shot Agnes must have gotten away before we rushed in. There was a door to the next room in the opposite wall. I supposed he had slipped through it when he heard us coming and the door closing behind him was what I heard. He didn't have time to fire again because of us. I didn't know if Agnes would survive but I was sure a second shot when she was down, like Frank Cervone had received, would have done her in.

—*ele*—

The ambulance rocked as we barreled through the streets. The wait had seemed interminable, but when they finally arrived the medics swiftly took over. They tightly bandaged Agnes, lifted her onto a stretcher and rushed back to the street. When we followed, they allowed Lizzie and me to climb in. With bells clanging, we sped to Cook County Hospital.

Inside, Agnes was whisked away. When I tried to reach Stephen, I was shocked to hear that he refused to come down to us. And we were forbidden to enter the section treating the influenza patients. I was so angry, I shivered. Lizzie put an arm on my shoulders and turned me away.

"Come along, Mother. We'll find Jack."

I looked back. They had taken Agnes away so I had no idea whether she would live. I dreaded facing Jack, but I let Lizzie lead me downstairs to the basement. At the bottom we were surrounded by shrouded corpses lining the hallway. Taking a deep breath, Lizzie hurried me down to Eli's office with the hanging artificial limbs. Jack was there.

He stood across the broad table from us. When we blurted out that Agnes had been shot, he turned white, and

Lizzie rushed around to his side and helped him sit on a stool.

"We found her in her studio at the Art Institute. They're working on her, but I called your father and he refused to come down. Jack, you've got to find him for me. Why wouldn't he come down?" I clenched my teeth so I wouldn't get hysterical. It was so unlike Stephen to refuse to come.

Bleary eyed, Jack asked, "Who did it? Who shot Agnes?"

"We don't know. He ran away. Why would anyone shoot her?" Lizzie asked.

Jack shut his eyes and clutched the edge of the table.

I looked around. "Where's Dr. Lieberman?"

Jack opened his eyes and looked at me across the space of the table. "I don't know. They said he was just here, but he's left again." He shook his head as if to clear his eyesight. Then he stood. "I have to go."

"Yes, go find out what's happening with Agnes," I said. "We asked but they couldn't tell us anything. And someone should contact her mother."

"I'll send a telegram," Lizzie said.

Jack looked at us blankly. I heard a noise behind me. A young man with a flourishing mustache pounded into the room followed by two uniformed men. I recognized him. He was a detective, one of Whitbread's colleagues.

"Dr. Chapman?" he asked.

Jack looked confused. "That's me."

The detective nodded to the policemen. "Search the place. Dr. Chapman, I need you to come to the station with me."

"What's this about?" I asked.

He looked at me. "Mrs. Chapman, we need to talk to you and your daughter. Miss Agnes Graham was shot at the Art Institute, and I'm charged with the investigation. Please come along."

"You don't think Jack had anything to do with that? He didn't know, we only just told him." I remembered Whitbread had gone to Wisconsin. If he were present, it would have been much easier to explain. We would spend hours at the Harrison Street station now with officers I barely knew. And we needed to know how Agnes was doing. I couldn't understand why Stephen refused to see me. If he were here at the hospital, I would be confident someone was making sure Agnes was getting the best treatment possible. But I hadn't been able to tell him.

One of the uniformed men took Jack's arm and herded him and Lizzie to my side of the room. The other man was rifling through papers and opening and shutting drawers when he exclaimed. We all stopped and looked across at him. He waved a gun in his hand. He sniffed the barrel. "Smells like it's been fired recently," he said.

I groaned. Jack's gun was finally found.

TWENTY-NINE

After several hours at the police station, they released Lizzie and me, but they kept Jack for interrogation. I tried to get them to contact Detective Whitbread, but they didn't know where he was. They ignored my information about Caroline Longman's family in Wisconsin.

As we left the station, Lizzie headed back to the hospital to find out how Agnes was doing and to make sure her mother had received the telegram. I hesitated.

"I have to find Dr. Lieberman," I told her.

"Mother, what good will that do?"

"He must know why that gun was in his office. Jack said he'd been there. Do you know where their lodgings are?" I asked.

She shook her head in disbelief at my stubbornness, I guess. But I had to do something useful. I couldn't sit around the hospital waiting and I was already hurt by Stephen's refusal to help. I couldn't stand a second rebuff, and I would make a spectacle of myself if I got really angry and stormed upstairs looking for him.

"I don't know where he lives, but I think on Saturdays he helps at Dr. Reitman's clinic. Jack told me," she said.

That was enough to give me a goal. I hurried off to Hull House. Someone there would know exactly where Reitman had his clinic. I'd knew that he hosted venereal disease clinics in Chicago jails, but he also had a private clinic on the south side. Syphilis and other venereal diseases were hidden problems that deeply embarrassed even the hoboes and prostitutes who sought him out. At Hull House, we saw much of the underside of life in a city, and sexual diseases were just one of the problems. I was not surprised to hear that people in upper-class society of Chicago also sought out Dr. Reitman. Disease has no respect for class.

I found the clinic in a brick building in the South Loop and climbed to the second floor. I recognized several of the men smoking in the corridor or hunched over in chairs of a waiting room as IWW men who'd been at the Dil Pickle. They were mostly large men who hulked over me as I passed through to the desk at the end of the room. I saw one woman. One smartly dressed middle-aged man looked out of place and when he saw me, he blushed, rose, and pushed his way out to the hoots of the workingmen. The woman behind the desk shook her head. "What do you want?" she asked.

I tried to reassure her that I was not prying. "I have no interest in Dr. Reitman's patients. I'm only looking for a Dr. Lieberman, who helps him. It's very important that I find him." Eli Lieberman must have put that pistol in the drawer at his office. I believed Jack when he said he knew nothing about it. I hated to think it of Eli, but if he *had* shot

Agnes Graham, I needed to make him turn himself in to the police. I could think of no reason why he would hurt Agnes, but Jack had taken his gun to protect himself and his roommate. Eli could have used it to shoot Agnes. Useless thoughts circled in my mind, and I couldn't still myself. I had to find Eli and make him tell the police what happened before they arrested Jack.

The woman ducked her head and led me through to a white painted room that smelled of bleach. My guide stepped across to a door and knocked. The door opened and Dr. Reitman came out with his arm around a pale young woman who clutched a shawl around her shoulders.

"Now, you must return for another treatment next week. You understand?"

She nodded and raised the shawl over her head before leaving. I bit my lip. She was a prostitute.

Dr. Reitman must have seen emotions pass across my face because his own hardened and he looked angry. "What do you want?" he asked.

I stood taller. "I'm looking for Dr. Lieberman. It's very important that I speak to him."

He glanced at the woman who had brought me in and told her to make the next patient wait. Then he opened the door and shooed me in. The room was being cleaned by a nurse. She bundled stained sheets into a wicker basket and moved a mop and pail beside the examination table to scrub the floor. I saw the massive back of Dr. Lieberman at a counter pouring boiling water on instruments in a tin pan. When he turned and saw me, he said, "Mrs. Chapman. How did you know to come here?"

"I've worked at Hull House for many years. They helped me find the clinic. Lizzie told me you worked with Dr. Reitman. I must talk to you, Dr. Lieberman."

"Hull House," Dr. Reitman snorted. "I might have known. Those do-gooders claim to have remedies for the suffering of these people, but there's more unemployment, delinquency, perversion, and police brutality than when they started. And they know it."

Being a member of the sociology department at the University of Chicago, I was aware that Dr. Reitman had a low opinion of academics and social workers. His burst of venom wasn't unexpected.

"They said you run a syphilis clinic," I said to reassure them. "It's known that you provide a drug treatment for it to all levels of society." Even members of Chicago's wealthy class were whispered to have consulted Chicago's Pox Doctor. No doubt the man who rushed away was an example.

Reitman tore off the stained white apron he wore. "Treatment. All that's needed for the treatment of syphilis is an understanding of venereal disease, and money to purchase soap and prophylactics. But that's too much for the dainty emotions of society. Ignorance is rampant." He waved an arm and stepped to the sink to wash his hands.

Eli Lieberman faced me. "What did you want from me, Mrs. Chapman?" The nurse had returned to her mop. They were used to Dr. Reitman's tirades.

"Agnes Graham's been shot—at the Art Institute. Lizzie and I got her to the hospital. The police found a gun in your office and took Jack for questioning. They're looking for you."

"I know nothing of a gun. I've been here all afternoon."

"It happened this morning. Jack said you left early. Did you take Jack's gun and shoot her?"

"What? Of course not. What gun? I had business." He clutched his artificial arm to his side with his good hand. His dark eyes darted around looking at the ceiling, the floor, everywhere but at me. I waited. It made him nervous. "If you must know, I went to Murphy's saloon to pay a debt."

"A gambling debt?"

He nodded. "Agnes was right, what she said about me and gambling. She made me feel bad about it, saying it in front of you and your daughter like that. I sold a couple of medical instruments and a microscope to pay them off. But I know nothing about a gun."

Dr. Reitman stomped over and put himself between me and Eli. "This interrogation is over. We have work to do. Get out."

Eli looked embarrassed by the rudeness.

"Eli, you must go to the police and tell them what you know." Reitman put a hand on the small of my back and urged me through the doorway, calling for one of the men as he did so. The man got up and passed me to go in. The door slammed behind him.

Had Cervone been dunning Eli for payment of gambling debts on behalf of the Murphys? Did Jack's friend and roommate kill the debt collector? Eli claimed he'd paid the debts. Where did he get the money? Was it really from pawning medical equipment?

As I passed through the crowded waiting room, I was aware of stares from the men. These were not avant-garde artists and writers. These were hard men who were angry about how society treated them. Hoboes and labor activists, prostitutes, and criminals from the underworld of the city. They seemed very threatening. Eli Lieberman was part of this world which was every bit as dangerous as the world of Big Mike Murphy. How had Jack and Lizzie become allied with people of this world? Did they know what they were getting into?

I was annoyed that Eli refused to come with me and embarrassed to be thrown out so quickly by Reitman. The police would find Eli soon enough. I wished Detective Whitbread was back from Wisconsin. I needed his help to protect Jack from suspicion. And poor Agnes. I hoped she would recover.

THIRTY

I stopped at the Harrison Street police station, but Jack was gone. He'd been released. I was relieved. I insisted they find Eli to question him, and I told them about the clinic. When I had done as much as I could, I went to the hospital where Lizzie was still waiting. Jack had not returned, and Stephen had not come down from the influenza wards. I pulled Lizzie into a corner, away from scurrying masked and aproned figures. The atmosphere was tinged with fear. Stretchers lined hallways in every direction except the wing where non-flu patients were treated.

"Mother, do you actually believe Eli shot Agnes?" Lizzie shook her head.

"I'm afraid Agnes could have known what Dr. Lieberman was involved in." I looked around but the medical staff were too busy to overhear us.

"What do you think he was involved in?" Lizzie frowned at me.

"I'm not sure but I'm afraid it has to do with the IWW. When I was at Hull House, I heard there are rumors of a labor action. There's going to be a protest about Haywood's sentencing. It could be dangerous." My worries were too vague, but I wanted to warn Lizzie against what might happen. Eli worked with Reitman who had been prosecuted for distributing birth control information. Authorities would look for any reason to arrest him. He was known to be the lover of Emma Goldman, an anarchist who was in prison for opposing the selective service draft, like the IWW leaders. I sympathized with many of their views, but I knew association with real anarchists required one to accept deadly actions like bombings. I could never accept that violence was necessary.

"Nonsense, Mother. Eli is more of a danger to himself than anyone else. He took Louis to a gambling den once. Louis was desperate for money to get away from Flora Murphy. He wanted to cut off his connection to the Murphy's altogether. He mentioned leaving town and starting fresh on the West Coast. When Agnes and Jack found out about the gambling, they argued with Louis. Jack warned Eli never to take Louis again."

Lizzie was more familiar with Jack and his friends than I had realized. Of course, Agnes was her friend before she introduced Jack. Still, I wondered how deeply involved she was in their lives. I didn't trust Eli Lieberman, no matter what she or Jack said. "I need to find Jack. The police let him go."

Lizzie told me that Agnes's mother was with her. The young woman was still unconscious although the doctors had finished treating her. There was nothing more the doctors could do. We had to wait for her body to heal if it could.

We thought there might be a clue as to where Eli lived in his basement office. Lizzie led the way. Bodies were stacked on the floor below stretchers with multiple bodies jammed together. They were covered by sheets, but they lined our route like walls being built around us. At the end of the corridor, men swathed in black carried stretchers upstairs and out a door to waiting crematorium vehicles. We hurried to the doorway of Eli's office. I kept my eyes from straying to the open doors of the morgue as we passed. I whispered a swift prayer, though.

Jack was not in the office, but Eli was there. He shuffled over uncertainly when he saw us, and he attempted to apologize to me for Reitman's dismissal.

I sighed. The police would be looking for him at the clinic based on what I'd told them.

"We need to find Jack," Lizzie said.

He looked down at the artificial leg she'd made for him and fingered it with his good hand. "I don't know where he is. I came to look for him, but he's gone."

"You should talk to the police," I said. "As I told you at the clinic, they think the gun they found in a drawer here may be the one that was used to shoot Agnes. They want to know where it came from."

He looked up. "I told you already, I know nothing about any gun."

I didn't believe him. "Jack took a gun from our home. He'd brought it back with him from France. He said he took it to your place in ease you needed to defend yourselves after the man Cervone was found dead in that alley. Are you saying he never showed you that gun? Why wouldn't he?"

Eli glanced at Lizzie and frowned. "No. He never showed me a gun. I swear it." He ignored me and stared at Lizzie. "How can you believe Jack, or I, would do anything to harm Agnes? Jack loves Agnes. He's my friend. She's my friend. I don't have that many friends. You think I would shoot one of them?" He shoved the artificial leg away, plopped down on a stool and took out his flask, raising it for a long gulp. I shook my head.

Lizzie stomped her foot. "Enough. Where's Jack?"

"I don't know!" Eli yelled, glaring at her.

"He lives with you. Take us there."

He took another drink.

"Tell us your address," I said. "So, we can look for him." I hoped Jack had gone to Eli's home to find his gun. That would prove it wasn't the gun found in Eli's office and wasn't the gun used to kill Cervone or to shoot Agnes. The thought made me more impatient to find my son.

When Eli turned his back to us Lizzie marched around the table and grabbed the flask from his hand. "Stop this. Take us to your place. Now."

He stood there, looming over her and for a minute I was afraid. He was such a mountain of a man. Reaching across her, he grabbed the artificial leg. "You promise to make me more of these, maybe I'll take you up on that." He grinned and I flinched. What was wrong with him?

Lizzie stood her ground. "Before you end up in prison or drink yourself to death? We'll see." She dropped the flask onto the table. "Take us to Jack. Now."

With a massive shrug of his large shoulders, he tucked the flask into a pocket. "It's Saturday." His words were slurred. "No cutting open today or on the Sabbath. Our days of rest."

Lizzie snorted and turned away. Eli shuffled over and led us out of the room.

THIRTY-ONE

W e followed Eli to his lodgings, which were in a Jewish neighborhood on the west side a ten-minute walk from Cook County Hospital. I was familiar with the area from surveys done by Hull House over the years. The area contained crumbling tenements interspersed with more substantial old houses and a few newer apartment buildings. The streets were empty on the Jewish Sabbath. Eli turned into a neat brick building. He led us through a tiled entryway and up stone stairs to the second floor.

Inside his apartment, the rooms had high ceilings with white moldings above dark mahogany furniture. Oriental rugs in deep reds and blues hid the floors. On one side stood a baby grand piano surrounded by bookcases. It was as if the room were cut in two, as the other half was littered with boxes, discarded newspapers, and overturned books. I saw a pile of paper fliers for an IWW demonstration in support of Bill Haywood. "We shall FIGHT until we WIN" was printed above a picture of the labor leader. So Eli did more than act in the plays at the Dil Pickle. He was involved with the militant group.

I wondered if Jack was also engaged in demonstrations supporting Haywood. I knew from experience that labor disputes were complicated issues. I didn't think my children realized how dangerous they could be. Haywood was a controversial figure, defended by the famous lawyer Clarence Darrow. But Darrow had disappointed me and many other people by the way he'd handled a case of bombings in Los Angeles. He'd gotten support by promising that the accused men were innocent, then later he turned around and had them plead guilty. The IWW was suspected of instigating murder, although the charges for that crime had been dismissed. The current legal issues had to do with actions to prevent the draft of men to fight in the war. I'd been a pacifist before the war, but I never approved of the use of violence for any cause. I doubted Jack and Lizzie were well informed about the dangers of sympathizing with IWW, the possibility of having to support or at least accept the consequences of violent actions. I was less sure about how involved Eli might be in illegal activities of some of the IWW members.

I turned away from the stack of fliers, feeling grim. The walls looked like pictures had hung there but were gone. Brass candlesticks stood on a wide table and the mantel of the fireplace. There was an old couch and two worn leather armchairs, but spaces for other furniture were empty. Under a shaded lamp on a low table there were pictures in silver frames. Family portraits, I assumed.

"Jack!" Eli yelled. When there was no answer, he sank into a leather armchair.

Lizzie walked to a wall opposite. One unframed picture—a blur of luscious greens and yellows—was hung haphazardly, while two charcoal sketches were taped to the wall. "That's one of Agnes's paintings."

I stepped over to look at the drawings. They were studies for Lizzie's figures in the Taft sculpture. "I gave those to Jack," she said.

Eli's head dropped down to his chest. "He's not here," he mumbled.

Lizzie went to the small table and picked up one of the photographs. Eli looked up and ran a hand over his face. "My parents' wedding," he said. "She died before I got back from France. My father died of the flu a month ago. We couldn't have a service. He was a doctor. Your father knew him."

Both of his parents were dead, soon after his experience in France. Disgusted as I was by my son's drunken gambler friend, I couldn't help seeing him in a different light. "I'm so sorry to hear that," I said.

"And the others?" Lizzie gestured at the little forest of picture frames.

"My younger brother died at the battle at Belleau Wood. My sister is married and lives in Cleveland. This is my parents' home. I couldn't give it up after..." He shook his head, like a dog who'd been in a puddle. "Jack's not here. I don't know where he goes. He's disappeared a lot lately. I thought it was to see Agnes, but he wasn't at the hospital."

Why had Jack disappeared a lot lately? I really needed to make him talk to me. I was exasperated.

Lizzie continued to explore the room. She nodded to the piano. "Who plays?"

Eli reached for his flask but changed his mind. Standing, he walked over to the shiny black instrument. Pulling out the bench, he sat and slammed his artificial limb on the keyboard.

Arms akimbo, Lizzie looked down at him. He shrugged, moved his artificial hand, and picked out a children's tune with his left hand. His hulking form hunched over the slim ivory keys.

"Where would Jack have hidden the gun if he brought it here?" I asked. Eli claimed Jack hadn't brought the gun to their rooms, but I hoped Jack just hadn't told his roommate about it. "Where was Jack sleeping?"

Eli pointed to a doorway. "Second door on the right is the room he's using."

I searched the room, rifling through Jack's sparse belongings. I could hear murmurs from Lizzie and Eli and an occasional note from the piano. I found nothing in Jack's drawers or under his bed. I sat on the bed in frustration when I heard them greet someone.

I hurried back to the front room. There was Jack. The others were telling him I was looking for him and asking about the gun. He dug in the pocket of his overcoat and pulled out a pistol.

"Here it is, Mother. See? Do you believe me now? I didn't shoot anyone and neither did Eli."

A knot clogged my throat. The gun. It wasn't the one found beside Frank Cervone's body, and it wasn't the one the police had taken from Eli's office drawer. Jack had the gun he had brought back from France. He hadn't used it to shoot anyone. "Oh, Jack. Thank God. But where have you been? We looked for you at the police station and the hospital. Where did you go?"

He looked confused. "I had to see to Agnes's mother. She was at the hospital. Agnes is still fighting for her life." He gulped. "But there's nothing her mother could do. I put her in a taxi to take her home. We'll know tomorrow whether Agnes will make it."

"But you weren't at the hospital when we looked for you."

He hesitated. "I was looking for you, to show you the gun," he said.

He was hiding something, but this wasn't the place to press him for an answer. He sank into the leather chair Eli had left.

"I should take this to the police, to show them," he said but he looked drawn, exhausted by the effort.

"No," I told him. "You can take it to Detective Whitbread, but he's gone to Wisconsin to look for Louis Graham's secretary. Wait for him to return, then I'll go with you to talk to him."

Jack sat up. "Wisconsin?"

"There's a young woman missing. We think she might know something about Louis Graham's death."

Jack bit his lip.

"I don't know what it has to do with the attack on Agnes," I admitted, "but both she and Agnes might know something about Louis Graham's death. Why else would someone attack Agnes?"

"But Flora Murphy shot Louis," Jack said. Eli and Lizzie watched silently. They all looked to me to explain.

"So, the police believe. But Whitbread is convinced Big Mike Murphy had something to do with it. I promised

Whitbread I'd go to the final day of the trial on Monday. We think Louis Graham's death may be related to the shooting at the Dil Pickle, and now that Agnes has been attacked, it's even more likely they're all connected. Wait for Whitbread to return. I'll go with you, and you'll give him the gun." I sounded more sure of myself than I was but I believed Whitbread would find the key to this mystery in his search for Caroline Longman.

THIRTY-TWO

I could do nothing more until Whitbread returned. I thought that if I took Jack to see him, and brought him the gun, it would prove, or at least make it seem reasonable that Jack was not the one who shot Cervone or Agnes. Jack and Lizzie returned to the hospital to remain at Agnes's bedside. I went home. At the hospital, I would be too tempted to storm upstairs looking for my husband.

Sunday was an empty day that week. Lizzie returned late Saturday night and left early in the morning. She hadn't seen her father. We hadn't attended church services for weeks, due to the epidemic. I bit my lip and said a few private prayers. When would this horrible sickness end? I longed to have my family back around me where they belonged.

I met with my neglected students on Sunday. It gave me some satisfaction to see them, even if we were all masked. I could hope that there was a future beyond this miserable time. But they told me of two more deaths, young people struck down, taken to the infirmary where the doctor could do nothing to stop the disease. How awful for their parents.

My last student seemed reluctant to leave. Something bothered her. I waited as she bit her lip. "Mrs. Chapman, I wonder if you've seen the *Daily News* today?" She held out a folded copy. As I took it, she rushed away, thanking me for the meeting.

Wondering what disturbed her so much, I unfolded the paper and on the bottom half saw articles about the Flora Murphy trial. One headline caught my eye. "Who Was the 'Tramp' With Louis Graham?"

"Testimony last week revealed there was an 'other woman' in the dead man's life. Who was it? Rumor has it a certain young female student of sculptor Taft took time off from her studio in Hyde Park to party with Louis Graham. The beauty in question has a brother courting Graham's sister and her mother was seen attending the trial. Was Graham getting ready to leave the ill-fated married woman, Flora, when he was shot? Suspense builds in the scandalous trial."

The article continued with more speculation. "B. Hecht" wrote it. And my student had recognized Lizzie and Jack. How could I have been so blind? When I'd heard the story about the jealous confrontation in the restaurant, I'd never dreamed Lizzie was the one who was attacked by Flora Murphy. I knew she and Jack had socialized with Louis, she'd told me about it, but somehow I never realized they were the ones who were with him in the restaurant for the distressing scene.

Everyone at the university would see it and know he described my children. I was furious. How dare the rambunctious reporter malign my family like that? I felt betrayed. I had treated the young man with courtesy, and this was how he repaid me.

I took an early train on Monday to attend the final day of the trial. I hadn't expected the crowds. Men and women surged into the courthouse, where uniformed officers attempted to keep them in line. People wanted to see and hear the final arguments firsthand. They jostled each other in the foyer waiting for the doors to the courtroom to open.

After asking a guard, I found the press room, a smoky office with ugly green walls of chipping paint. Two tables with telephones cluttered the room. It was a meager concession by the authorities to the power of the press. A half dozen young men played rummy at one table while another man strummed a banjo in the corner. A short man in shirtsleeves and fedora, smoking a cigar strode around the room, talking about making money in Florida. Heads turned when I entered.

"Mr. Hecht, I want to speak with you," I announced.

He leapt to his feet, careful to lay his cards face down. "Mrs. Chapman, how nice to see you." When I tried to indicate he should follow me out of the room, he said. "We can talk here. We're among friends." He introduced the men although I was not listening. They perked up like thirsty plants under a stream of water. Anything to relieve the boredom.

My stomach burned and I felt heat rising to my face. "How dare you implicate my children in the affairs of Flora Murphy and Louis Graham?" I demanded. "I was at the trial last week. Their names were not mentioned."

"Oh, that's what's got your dander up. Why? Didn't they tell you about it? I had it from a very good source that Miss Chapman and her brother were there with the Grahams when that scene went down. Are you saying they weren't?"

I couldn't admit that I didn't know, so his question only made me angrier. "You have no right to slur their names like that."

"Freedom of the press, Mrs. Chapman. Besides, I *didn't* actually use their names." He grinned, infuriating me. Seeing me on the verge of tears in my frustration, suddenly he turned contrite. "I'm sorry it upset you. But don't worry. It'll be forgotten tomorrow. Isn't that true, men?" He turned to the others. They seemed gleeful at his predicament, but they nodded. I could see they thrived on drama and waited for an explosion from me.

Hecht was ready with a distraction. "What about this Cervone shooting?" he asked, pulling out a notebook. "You're working with Whitbread on that, aren't you? What do you say to the rumors that the IWW men are trying to buy guns for an action?"

"What?" The other men were alert. "Hey, what've you got on the IWW, Hecht?" one of them asked.

He licked his lips. "It's to support Bill Hayward. He's out on bail they raised for him by borrowing, but they expect him to get twenty years for obstructing the draft. They're supposed to be planning a big demonstration against it. And I heard they'll be carrying guns." He looked at me.

"I know nothing about it," I said. And if I did know anything I wouldn't tell Hecht after he exposed my children to public scorn. I remembered the fliers at Eli's apartment. I should tell Whitbread about the rumor, but he was still in Wisconsin. Perhaps Jack Jones and the other IWW men had borrowed money to buy guns. They could have owed money to Cervone or his employers.

A clerk stuck his head in the room. "Trial to start in ten minutes."

The men jumped up and brushed past me to the door. Hecht stopped, fingering his hat. "Sorry, Mrs. Chapman. But really, I guarantee no one will remember that piece next week. Don't worry." He grinned.

The sly little worm hurried away as I fumed. Pain like a sharp icicle struck my heart to hear my daughter called a tramp by the cheating wife of the gambling king. How had we failed our children that they could be in such peril? Lizzie was painted as the object of Flora's jealousy and Jack had yet to prove his gun had not been used to kill. I followed them through the doorway hoping that I would hear Flora Murphy convicted.

THIRTY-THREE

The hallway was full. Everyone in the crowd wore white cotton masks, but I took a step back, reluctant to be so close to so many people. I had promised Whitbread to attend, but I was having second thoughts, when I felt a hand on my elbow. "Mrs. Chapman, come along with me, won't you?"

Of course, Fitz would have another way in. He led me around the corner to a door covered by a guard. The man nodded to Fitz. This must be how the lawyers and judges avoided the crowds. Fitz led me down a corridor and through another doorway until suddenly we were entering the court room from a side door. They hadn't opened the doors at the back of the room to the public yet, and Fitz settled me in a chair behind the defense table where Flora Murphy sat with her nurse. Her lawyer, Colonel Willis, was positioning her so the jury would have a good view. He hoped to gain sympathy for the poor fainting woman. I shook my head at the performance.

I thanked Fitz. He pursed his lips and gave me a pained smile in response. The doors opened with a swishing sound and the public piled in. People chattered and rushed for seats. The same group of women in swank hats and furs took the first rows behind the prosecution. It was still cold outside.

Judge and jury entered. Looking at the twelve men, I believed they would be influenced by Flora's weak and willowy figure. She and her lawyer played to their instincts to protect the shattered woman.

The prosecutor began final arguments. He practically sneered at the defense table as he painted a picture of a craven jealous woman who seduced a younger man and then shot him when he threatened to leave her.

Then the wily prosecutor reminded the jury how the defendant's stepson, Malcolm Murphy had testified to the woman's jealousy, and how she had made a scene at a restaurant.

I ground my teeth. Fitz put a big hand over mine and squeezed. Of course, he would have seen the newspaper article and recognized Lizzie and Jack. I bit my lip to keep from speaking out.

The prosecutor mentioned the racehorse letter from Flora that showed her jealousy of another woman, and he mentioned the gun Flora had purchased. He claimed the dead man's wound showed he was sitting down when he was shot, ridiculing the defendant's claim there was a struggle for the gun. He reminded them that Malcolm had rushed downstairs after the shooting to find Flora collapsed beside the dead man with the gun on the floor.

Finally, he warned the jury not to be taken in by the "flimsy oratory" of the famous Colonel Willis who, he assured them, was practicing for a run for the governor, using the publicity of the trial to start his campaign.

Colonel Willis sat back in his chair with a leg extended during the prosecutor's rampage. He looked handsome in his well-fitting suit, silk tie, and polished boots. He patted the hand of his client before rising to present his argument.

Strolling over to the jury box, he shook his head. "The prosecution is wrong. Wrong, wrong, wrong. We won't be claiming that Flora Murphy shot Louis Graham in a fit of insanity, because she never did it at all. She is innocent. It's a hard thing for the dead man's family to hear, we know it, but he was a blackmailer and a liar who was about to be exposed. He tried to kill Flora Murphy to keep her from revealing his infamy and, in the struggle, he was killed."

They weren't denying Big Mike knew about the relationship, but they weren't suggesting he had anything to do with the death. The defense also claimed that Louis couldn't have been shot sitting down because his body was found prone on the floor and the shot had killed him immediately. Flora, the wilting flower at the defense table, couldn't have moved him from the chair. I realized that the defense had never called Flora Murphy to the witness stand. They wanted the jury only to see, not to hear the accused woman. It was a carefully contrived defense.

Colonel Willis didn't try to defend Flora's affair with the younger man, he only quoted the biblical phrase about throwing the first stone. He said, "There is blackmail in this case. There are other things that are bad. But this man and this woman were not always bad. There is evidence that she, at least, wanted to reform. It was the effort of a woman to lead a wayward boy back to redemption, but, alas, he wouldn't be led. The only question is whether she killed him. The answer is no. *He* assaulted her, and *he* had the weapon. Her maid testified that she had nowhere to conceal the pistol on her person. The prosecution claims the defendant purchased a gun, but they never proved it was delivered to her. The prosecutor has accused us of perfidy, but the state has been guilty of unparalleled malice against this woman." He waved a hand at Flora, a delicate figure collapsed now in the arms of the nurse who was barely able to hold her up.

When the defense attorney bowed to the jury and sat down, the prosecutor jumped up. He was allowed a rebuttal. He was rattled. "Just more of this hot air dispenser, this pettifogger who is trying to be elected governor of this great state. We have shown you the bribes offered to the defense witnesses, don't forget that, and don't forget there is an ongoing investigation into potential perjury. And don't forget that this woman admitted she killed Louis Graham when she entered the jail but, as soon as Big Mike Murphy arrived, everything changed. Suddenly it was all the fault of the dead man. Don't believe it!

"You have heard oratory. You have heard word painting, but gentlemen, keep this in mind. Who killed Louis Graham? Louis Graham had broken off from his 'favorite' and that day his 'favorite' went to his office for a final accounting. Put that feeling of sympathy the defense has tried to make you feel for the defendant toward poor Louis Graham who had a right to live and enjoy his life. Remember the mandate from Almighty God 'Thou shalt not kill.'"

What a sordid mess. The prosecutor's argument had become a rant and I could see sympathy for the wilting Flora Murphy in the eyes of the jurymen. The judge instructed the jury, then we all stood while he left the room. As the crowd began to exit, I sat back down. Beside me, I felt Fitz hesitate then sit back down himself.

THIRTY-FOUR

Fitz gently touched my shoulder. "Emily, we must leave. They'll let us know when the jury has reached a decision."

I looked up at his worried face. "Yes." I felt around for my purse. As I turned to the back of the room, I saw Detective Whitbread standing by the doorway waiting for me. How much had he heard? And what had he found out in Wisconsin? The lawyers never mentioned Caroline Longman at the scene of Louis Graham's death. I turned to Fitz. "Where was Michael Murphy? He wasn't here."

Fitz frowned when he saw Whitbread. "Big Mike is very ill. He's been bedridden for a week. People don't want to believe it, but this trial has broken his heart."

I doubted Whitbread would believe it. I hurried to the door to find out what he had learned in Wisconsin. But his eyebrows rose at my companion. He wouldn't speak in front of Fitz. I was sure of that.

"Mrs. Chapman, I wonder if you could come to my office. I have several matters to discuss. I'll ask the clerk to let us know when the jury has a verdict."

"Yes." I turned to Fitz. "Thank you, Mr. Fitzgibbons. If you'll excuse me, I have students to supervise at the detective's office." Fitz's face reddened, but he nodded and walked away.

At the police station, we sent my two students away and closed the door of Whitbread's office. "Did you find Miss Longman?" I asked.

"I found her family. She ran away to them, as we thought, but they refused to take her in."

"Even if she was in danger?" I couldn't believe it.

"They live on a farm. They're very religious. It would seem their daughter ran away to the city in the first place to escape a rather strict set of rules. When she attempted to return, they scolded her and drove her off. They quoted a lot of scripture about sin and damnation. They refused to speak her name, and claimed they had no daughter, that she was dead to them."

"How cruel. You don't think she really *is* dead, do you?"

He shrugged. "Wherever she is, it's not on that farm. I could find no one else who would admit they'd seen her. We have to assume she returned to the city if she's still alive."

"Fitz says Big Mike Murphy is very ill. Perhaps he's lost interest in Caroline Longman." I hoped that was the case.

"I noticed he was not in the courtroom," Whitbread said. "I took a train back this morning, so I missed the final arguments. What happened?"

There was no point trying to hide my concerns from Whitbread. "Lizzie was mentioned as someone Flora Murphy had accosted in public. They didn't name her, but it was clearly Lizzie. That reporter Hecht made that clear in his newspaper yesterday. The prosecutor claimed Flora was deeply jealous of Louis Graham. But the defense counsel argued that Graham was blackmailing her and that her husband told her to get back her letters and stop paying him money. They claim Graham attacked her with the pistol and, in the struggle, he was shot."

"No suggestion that anyone else was present?" he asked.

"Not at all." I knew Whitbread had hoped to find a witness who would connect Big Mike or one of his henchmen to the death of Louis Graham.

He grunted. "Murphy's paying her lawyer. I'm sure he insisted there be no hint of anyone else there. It's too late now. The jury is out."

I told him about the attack on Agnes Graham. "Do you think it had anything to do with her testimony in the trial?"

He nodded vigorously. "Surely Miss Graham does not know many people who would shoot a gun at her. It has to be connected to Murphy and his crew."

"The police found a gun in Eli Lieberman's office while you were away. They think it was used to shoot Agnes. But Jack showed me his own pistol. It wasn't the one found in Eli's office."

Whitbread looked disturbed. "I'll talk to the detectives. Your son should have brought the weapon in. We can't be sure which weapon was used."

"It was my fault. I told him to wait for your return."

I thought about Jack's admission that he'd been at the Monadnock Building the day Louis Graham was shot. I should tell Whitbread. But first, I told him Hecht's news about the IWW men of the Dil Pickle hoarding weapons for a demonstration.

"I have heard the same rumors. They want to do something about Bill Hayward's sentencing hearing. That's coming next week."

The telephone rang. It was the courthouse. The jury was returning. Whitbread looked surprised. "That was fast," he commented.

I wondered how the jury had decided so quickly. Whitbread believed Big Mike had sent someone to shoot Louis Graham, but the jury hadn't heard any evidence that even suggested that scenario. Perhaps it was obvious to them that Flora had fired the shot.

Before we left the station, Whitbread stopped to confer with the detective who'd been assigned to Agnes's shooting. He was very quiet when he returned to me.

At the courthouse, Whitbread hustled me through a door for witnesses and we took seats near the back. Voices and the rustling of the crowd stopped for a minute as Flora Murphy, dressed in black mourning, walked down the aisle supported by her middle-aged nurse who was all in white. Flora looked removed from it all, staring into the distance. She sat straight-backed. Her lawyer, Colonel Willis, leaned forward, elbows on the desk. Everyone rose when the judge returned, and he ordered in the jury.

The judge asked if they'd reached a verdict. A tall gray-haired man rose and answered that they had. He handed a paper to the clerk, it was read by the judge and returned. "Read the verdict, Mr. Clerk."

The crowd hushed as the clerk took a breath. "We, the jury, find the defendant not guilty."

The women in the front sprang to their feet clapping. The nurse sobbed against Flora Murphy's shoulder, while the accused woman looked unmoved. I heard a noise and turned around to see Malcolm Murphy rush out of the room. The judge called for order. Colonel Willis thanked the court and finally Flora collapsed weeping, gathered in by her nurse. The judge adjourned and we rose as he left. I thought of poor Agnes Graham clinging to life with her mother at her bedside.

Detective Whitbread raised an eyebrow. He looked grim, nodding toward the defense table where Fitz was congratulating Colonel Willis. "They got the result they wanted," he said.

THIRTY-FIVE

Outside, the prosecutor was surrounded by a crowd of reporters. Hecht winked at me. The prosecutor criticized the defense attorney. "The speech made by counsel for the defense might be the most eloquent ever heard in this courtroom, but it was also the most unfair. It was an argument not on fact but on fancies. The same gentleman with his power of word-painting could pick up a slimy reptile and make it beautiful to you. But I would see only a snake. You're reporters, not orators. You deal in facts. You can recognize a snake when you see one." He went on to accuse the defense of bribing witnesses.

As Whitbread ushered me away, I thought to myself that I agreed the whole story was a slimy one. I hated that my son and daughter had been anywhere near such treachery. I wondered if the acquittal of Flora Murphy meant that City Hall would allow Whitbread to investigate further. I doubted it. They wanted it all to go away.

In some ways, that would be good. I'd never told Whitbread that Jack was in the Monadnock Building that day, and I couldn't bear to see Lizzie's involvement with

Louis Graham publicized. But Whitbread was a dog with a bone. Until he found out what happened to Caroline Longman, he wouldn't rest.

We were joined by the other detective and two uniformed men. Whitbread led us away from the crowd, then turned to me. "Mrs. Chapman, where is your son right now?"

I drew in a sharp breath. Surely, he wasn't going to arrest Jack. But the presence of the uniformed men suggested that might be his plan. Did he believe that Jack's gun was used to shoot Cervone or Agnes? I blamed myself for telling Jack to wait for Whitbread's return to give his gun to the police. I swallowed. "I think he's at the morgue in Cook County Hospital."

"Please come with us." Whitbread led us to a police wagon on a side street. After a short ride, they helped me out of the back of the wagon. I saw the massive stone face of the hospital. We marched to Eli Lieberman's basement office beside the morgue.

The door was open. Inside, Eli and Lizzie were bent over a man who sat on a chair. Behind them the large table held tools including a saw and screwdrivers. They were adjusting a leather harness.

"There. Is that better?" Eli asked. He bent forward to touch the man's knee.

He was young, perhaps twenty. He grimaced but followed the frown with a grin up at Lizzie. "Much better. Thank you, miss. I can't wait to tell the guys who made my new leg."

The group looked up at our approach and I saw Jack was on the other side of the room, sitting on a stool by the table.

"Hello, Mother." Lizzie looked confused by the men trailing after me. I saw Jack stand up.

"Mrs. Chapman," Eli said. "We're just fitting the new leg for Private Toomey, here. He ran into enemy fire at the Marne, and he's been hobbling around on these." He grabbed a set of crutches and held them up. "He's the lucky recipient of Miss Chapman's first sculpture and he's a happy man, aren't you, Private?"

"You bet, sir." The young man gave us a sunny smile and reached out for a cane that Lizzie held. "Here goes." He stood up, a little shaky, but took two steps. "Yes, ma'am, that's just hunky-dory."

Lizzie and Eli had noticed Whitbread and the other policeman, so they helped the private out the far door and Eli closed it and returned.

I looked across at Jack. My heart was beating but I tried to slow my breathing. Whatever happened we would deal with it. I wondered how long it would take to contact Clarence Darrow, the lawyer who'd tried to help my dead son, Tommy, when he was in trouble.

Whitbread stepped forward. "Dr. Chapman, your mother told me you have been able to produce a pistol that you brought back from France. It's her contention that your possession of the gun now means it couldn't have been used in the attack on Miss Agnes Graham. Do you have that pistol?"

Jack's face was white, but he stepped to a side cabinet and opened it. Whitbread nodded to the uniformed men, and they went to look over my son's shoulder. Jack glanced back at me in shock. Did our old friend Whitbread, who'd known my family since before my children were born, really believe Jack could have shot Agnes? I shook my head in disbelief. I didn't know what to say to Jack.

He pulled the pistol from his medical bag. It was wrapped in cloth. He handed it to one of the policemen who brought it to Whitbread. Unwrapping the gun, he showed it to the other detective and nodded his head. Then he took a step forward to face Eli.

"Dr. Eli Lieberman, I am arresting you for the murder of Francis James Cervone and the attempted murder of Agnes Graham." He motioned to an officer who put handcuffs on Eli.

"But why would Eli shoot anyone?" Lizzie spoke first. "He'd never hurt Agnes. What are you doing?"

Whitbread grunted and motioned for the officers to take Eli. "We have a witness who saw Dr. Lieberman argue with Cervone at the Dil Pickle and another who saw him with a gun that night. We believe Miss Graham witnessed something incriminating. We'll know more when she's well enough to speak." I saw Jack flinch. The doctors weren't sure Agnes would pull through. "Dr. Lieberman offered an alibi for the time of Miss Graham's shooting, but that has been found to be inaccurate and the gun we believe was used in that shooting was found here, in Lieberman's office."

One officer held Eli's arms while another rifled through his pockets. He found something and raised a hand holding a scalpel. He placed it on the table, then he withdrew Eli's silver flask from another pocket and put it on the table.

"We do autopsies," Jack said. "That's why he has a scalpel." But I didn't think the doctors normally kept such implements in their pockets. Whitbread motioned to the officers, and they took Eli's arms to lead him away.

Eli squirmed to look at Lizzie. "So sorry to disappoint," he said. "I always do, you know." They half dragged him through the door. Whitbread and the other detective followed.

"Oh, Eli," Jack moaned. "What have you done?"

THIRTY-SIX

N o. I don't believe it," Lizzie said. She stood beside the table, turning the scalpel over and over. "He'd never hurt Agnes."

Jack had his head in his hands as if it hurt him to think. "You haven't seen him in his blackest moods." He stepped over and took the scalpel from her hands. "Do you know why he kept this on his person? He told me once it was in case it got too bad. He knew with a flick he could cut his jugular and be done with it." Jack dropped the knife as if it were burning his fingers.

"But why would he kill other people?" Lizzie asked. She stared at the scalpel as if it were a snake, liable to attack any minute. "I don't believe he'd kill for money. If he owed money for gambling and Cervone was going to hurt him, it would be self-defense, wouldn't it? But if he was so suicidal, why didn't he just let Cervone kill him? Do you really believe that he'd kill a man to escape debts and then shoot Agnes because she saw something? It doesn't make sense."

"It doesn't make sense to us," I said. "You would never shoot someone, so you can't imagine anyone else doing such a deed." I'd always been surprised by the motives that drove the murderers I met while working with Whitbread. "Dr. Lieberman seems very close to Jack Jones, Ben Reitman, and the IWW men at the Dil Pickle," I said. "There's reason to believe they may have owed money that Cervone was sent to collect. It's rumored they'll make a lot of trouble when Bill Haywood comes up for sentencing next week."

They looked at me blankly. My children didn't know about any planned labor action. But how well did they know their friend Eli?

"Some people will do unexpected things for a cause they believe in," I told them.

Lizzie stood shaking her head as if to clear it. "I don't believe it."

Jack looked surprised and confused, as if he'd reached a dead end and didn't know where to turn.

I told Jack. "Go up and get your father. Tell him he must come down. I need to talk to him." I was so relieved that Whitbread had not taken my son away in handcuffs that I almost felt lightheaded. But I was deeply worried by all I was learning about the lives of our children and the friends they associated with. Stephen was always stronger than me. I needed his strength to help them.

Jack left on my errand. I could see he agreed with me that we needed his father at this crisis. Lizzie dropped down to a bench by the wall.

"Lizzie, I was at the trial of Flora Murphy today. When the prosecutor was summing up, he said that Flora Murphy was jealous of a woman. I know he was talking about your friendship with Louis Graham. He claimed that she even tried to assault you publicly at a restaurant. Is that true? Why did you never tell us?" I didn't mention the newspaper article. If she hadn't seen it, she wouldn't be as hurt by it as I was.

Lizzie looked up as if through a fog. "Flora Murphy? Oh, yes, she did yell at me one time. We were with Jack and Agnes at the Berghoff. She's a very foolish woman. She followed Louis sometimes. He couldn't let her know when he went out with anyone else. He tried to hide it, but I think he was afraid of her. She was quite wild that night." Lizzie frowned. "I don't see how a woman who claims to love a man can stoop to doing him so much harm. Why was she like that?"

"Lizzie, were you in love with Louis Graham?"

"What? No, I told you. I felt sorry for him. He was trapped by that woman. But love? No, he never stirred my heart." She looked up, surprised. Then I saw her gaze at Eli's silver flask. I hoped her heart was not stirring for Jack's very disturbed friend. I was silent, unsure what to say to her. I hoped I was jumping to false conclusions.

Jack hurried in. He held a sheaf of papers, and he was totally white in the face. I wondered if he had stopped to check on Agnes but, when I asked, he looked at me blankly. "No, I saw Father." He gulped. "He said he can't come down. He's very, very sorry but he begs that you will take his report to the committee meeting at the Sherman House tonight. He's supposed to go but he's swamped. He promises he'll see you tomorrow and you can tell him about the meeting."

I took the papers he shoved at me and sighed. "Yes, of course, I'll take them. I was supposed to observe but I was going to skip the meeting. Is it very bad up in his ward?"

"It's terrible," Jack said. I was shocked to see him so unnerved. He'd been working in the hospital, dealing with the bodies of the dead for a month, and he'd seen awful sights on the battlefield, yet he looked shocked. I wondered if the flu was getting worse.

"There's something else, Mother," Jack said. He went to his medical bag and pulled out a leather-covered book. "Would you give this to the police? It's Louis Graham's account book for the Liberty Bond drive. It proves he didn't steal the money." He sighed. "Agnes really wanted to clear his name from that accusation."

I noticed he used the past tense for Agnes. He must know that her condition was very bad. I felt pain in my heart for him. "I'm so sorry, Jack. Flora Murphy was acquitted this afternoon. The jury believed that Louis Graham was killed in a struggle for the gun. Detective Whitbread has already been forbidden to investigate the case. With a jury verdict decided, City Hall won't want to reopen any investigation of Louis Graham's death. I don't think Whitbread could use the accounts now. The trial is over."

His eyes glittered with tears. "Please, Mother. I promised Agnes."

I took the account book from him. "Yes, of course. I'll give it to the police anyway." How had Agnes come by the account book? Had her brother hidden it at home?

"What about Eli?" Lizzie asked faintly.

Oh, no. Perhaps my assumptions weren't so far off the mark. Lizzie seemed to care a lot about Eli Lieberman.

"We should try to get Clarence Darrow to represent him," Jack said. I could understand why he felt obliged to help his friend and roommate.

"I can do that," Lizzie said. I wasn't happy that she was so eager to help Eli. But to argue with her would be a mistake. With effort, I kept my mouth shut.

"I have work here," Jack said. "You need to go to the meeting. For Father." He gulped. "Lizzie, stay a minute and I'll tell you what Darrow needs to know about Eli."

I was glad they weren't paralyzed by what was happening. I left them reluctantly, planning to meet Lizzie at home later that night.

Thirty-Seven

A t the Sherman House Hotel, the influenza committee met in a private room. This time, there were state authorities in addition to the city delegation led by Dr. Robertson. I looked at him with new eyes. I remembered what Stephen had told me of how he'd driven the former health official to suicide and how he thought stopping bathing could cure tuberculosis.

The head of the state department of health reported that the epidemic was receding. The death rate and new cases had shrunk fourteen percent in the past three days. Nonetheless, the state official said that "places of amusement" would not reopen yet. Local health departments could pass judgement on when reopening could happen, but plans would need to be reviewed by the state and agreed to.

I thought Stephen would be encouraged to learn that Robertson would need to convince state officials before opening up the city. I wanted to tell the committee about the piles of corpses at Cook County morgue, and the lack of coffins, but I quietly presented Stephen's written report along with others from various hospitals. They would be compiled by the state.

Dr. Robertson rose, clearing his throat. "The death rate in Chicago yesterday showed a marked decrease from last week. There were four hundred and twenty-eight deaths compared to four hundred and sixty-eight last week. The previous week the number was over five hundred, so you can see the decreasing rate."

There was a shuffling of papers and an air of anticipation in the room. I thought they were expecting Robertson to suggest opening sooner, but he introduced a man from the Chicago Surface Lines instead. He reported there were a lot of streetcars not operational due to the lack of six hundred workers out sick with the flu. When Dr. Robertson proposed a ten o'clock curfew, I saw Fitz move uncomfortably in his chair. He stood up.

"I'm here on behalf of Mayor Thompson and City Hall," he said. He frowned over a paper report of the latest statistics that had been distributed. "The mayor and all of us are very thankful for the hard work this committee and all of your staff have been doing. We're encouraged and relieved by the decrease in infections. I've been authorized to announce that the city will begin lifting restrictions on November fourth. Because of the downward trend, we're confident the hard work of getting the city back on its feet must begin as soon as possible. The mayor will be announcing this date along with the decreased number of deaths to the press tomorrow."

There was a stunned silence. This wasn't what was expected. The numbers were decreasing, but the bodies were still piling up in the Cook County morgue. Stephen would be furious.

The state health inspector objected. "Any changes in restrictions need to be submitted to the state for approval," he pointed out. "I told you that moments ago."

Fitz fiddled with the papers in front of him. Dr. Robertson jumped up. "The city will submit any necessary documentation in a timely fashion," he said. "Don't worry. We've got it all in hand."

My mouth dropped open. Robertson had quickly changed his tune.

I was appalled. I had to speak up. "Dr. Chapman was unable to attend this meeting due to the severity of the crisis in the Cook County Hospital," I said. "I'm here only as an observer for Hull House, but I know Dr. Chapman would argue that November fourth is too soon to drop the restrictions. There aren't even enough coffins for those who've died already."

Dr. Robertson was annoyed by my interruption. I thought it had more to do with the fact that I was a woman speaking up, than that Stephen would have disagreed. Robertson himself had started the meeting by emphasizing the ongoing crisis, but he'd caved as soon as Fitz spoke of City Hall's determination to start ignoring the influenza. As if that would make it go away!

"Thank you for that *opinion*," Robertson said. "I'm sure the officials at City Hall will take Dr. Chapman's views into account. But I think we can all agree that we have time to improve the situation before the proposed deadline."

Men from other local cities and towns spoke up to suggest they would not be ready so soon. I was helpless. My status was that of an observer. I'd already gone beyond that role. I had to sit and listen in silence till the meeting ended with another admonition by the state health director that plans should be submitted for review. I very much doubted that Fitz and Robertson would comply.

As people began to leave, Fitz appeared at my side. "I'm sorry, Emily. I understand that Stephen would object, but the mayor is determined to get the city moving again."

"People are still dying, Fitz. Stephen couldn't come because they are so overwhelmed at Cook County."

"I know that, and I promise we'll get them every resource they need. No one wants this to end as much as the mayor."

"No one except the doctors and nurses risking their own lives to try to treat the sick," I insisted.

"I know. And we're grateful to them." I began to move away, but Fitz stepped in front of me. "I wonder if I could ask you for a favor," he said.

"What?"

"It's Flora Murphy. I know you were interested in the trial. Big Mike is truly very ill. I've agreed to take Mrs. Murphy to his bedside tomorrow, and I wonder if you could accompany us? She's been staying at a hotel in the Loop during the trial. I'd pick you up at your house in a motorcar tomorrow morning."

I was surprised by the request. Why me? "Oh, you want a chaperone? After all that was revealed during the trial about Flora Murphy, you think you need a chaperone, Fitz? Really?"

He looked pained. "In the circumstances, it seems even more important to be discreet," he said.

Discreet? This woman who had shot her lover had also accused my own daughter of stealing him away. My face burned. But then I thought of Whitbread and how he'd been prevented from investigating the crime. Would an ailing Big Mike and a disgraced Flora reveal what really happened that day? If they did, Whitbread might finally know the truth. Perhaps they knew where Caroline Longman had gone and whether she was still alive. I had to find out if I could, so I agreed to go with Fitz.

THIRTY-EIGHT

When I got to the kitchen in the morning, Lizzie had already prepared tea and toast. She was surprised to hear that Fitz would be taking me to the Murphy house in Oak Park.

"You're going with Flora Murphy?" she asked.

"As a sort of chaperone, I suppose."

Lizzie snorted. "How can she worry about her reputation after that trial? Surely, it's too late now. Poor Agnes. She'll be furious when she hears Flora was acquitted." She stopped. "I just hope she lives to hear about it."

"I hope so, too. I'm only going along to see if Flora or her husband say anything about what really happened the day Louis Graham died." Of course, there was no reason for them to reveal their secrets to me. The effort was probably hopeless. But, with the trial over and Flora released, I thought there was at least a chance Flora or Mike might say something to throw a light on what had really happened that day. I never fully believed the scenarios offered by either the prosecution or the defense. There was something missing.

Lizzie raised an eyebrow.

"It's for Detective Whitbread," I said. "He's trying to find out where Louis's secretary, Caroline Longman, has gone and whether she witnessed what happened that day."

"Whitbread," Lizzie scoffed. "Flora Murphy goes free, and Eli Lieberman's arrested. The authorities are wrong about all of this." She shook her head. "I'll find Mr. Darrow and take him to Eli. But then I want to go to Agnes's work area at the Art Institute. Whoever shot her must have wanted something from her, don't you think? She must have evidence against someone for them to want to get rid of her, and our presence could have prevented him from finding it. There might be something there."

Lizzie was desperate to help Eli. Whitbread claimed that Eli shot Agnes because she saw him with the dead man at the Dil Pickle, not because she had evidence of wrongdoing. I didn't contradict Lizzie because she was so determined to prove him wrong. But if Agnes saw something that night, or had some evidence, why hadn't she told the police already? And if Eli hadn't done it, where did the gun they found in his office come from?

Lizzie sensed my skepticism. "Mother, I know Eli didn't shoot Agnes. He couldn't. There has to be another explanation."

Oh, Lizzie, be careful of your heart. "How is Agnes?" I asked.

"Still fighting for her life. We were preparing for an exhibition next week, did you know? It's not an official one. A sculptor friend has rented a place to show pieces too outrageous for the stuffy academics at the Art Institute. I know it means a lot to Agnes to have her work included.

I want to pack up the pieces she meant to show. There's nothing else I can do for her now." Lizzie spread her hands helplessly. I was glad she could do something useful for Agnes because I expected her search for evidence to save Eli Lieberman would fail.

I took one of her hands. "I'm sure she'd appreciate that. I'll come help you after I go to Oak Park." I almost wished I hadn't agreed to go, Agnes's fight for life was more important than the sordid affair between her brother and Flora Murphy. But it was too late to change my mind. We heard a knock at the door, and I gathered my things, including the account book Jack had pleaded with me to take to the police. With the trial over and Flora found not guilty, we probably wouldn't be able to clear Louis Graham's reputation, but I had agreed to try.

At the door, Fitz ushered me into the back of his large motorcar and told the driver the address. I was a bit uncomfortable knowing I only agreed to come because I wanted information.

"Fitz, I was very shocked to hear that Mrs. Murphy called my daughter a tramp. You saw that newspaper article. Anyone would recognize Lizzie. Flora Murphy publicly accused my Lizzie of a romantic attachment to Louis Graham. Lizzie assures me they were only friends because she and Louis's sister were close," I said grimly.

Beside me, Fitz sat forward. "Oh, I'm sure that was just the prosecutor's attempt at dramatics." But my friend from City Hall still defended the accused woman. "You must have seen that Flora was in a state of shock through most of the trial. She was out of her mind even before that. She barely knew what was going on. She had to move out of her home because of the publicity. She's had a very bad time, Emily."

I looked at him. Sure enough, he was in one of his gloomy romantic states. I was sure he'd brought me along to try to gain my sympathy for the woman he admired. I had no patience with his imagined heartache.

"Fitz, the woman seduced a schoolboy then carried on with him for years before finally being the death of him." I hadn't given up Whitbread's theory that one of Big Mike's henchmen fired the shot, but Flora Murphy was still responsible for the young man's death. "You're taking her to see her sick husband. This is not a woman you should admire and wish for. Wake up from this dream of her. She's not the poor injured angel that you," (and the men of the jury, I was sure) "think of as innocent."

Fitz lowered his eyes and rubbed his hands over his face "I can't help feeling for her, Emily. She's so young and tragic."

I suppressed a sharp comment. Fitz was an irredeemable romantic and always had been. I should know he was too old to change now.

Luckily, we stopped at a building in the Loop before I could open my mouth, and Fitz left to get Flora Murphy. He brought her back, leaning on his arm, and placed her next to me as carefully as if she were made of fine china. I thought of her more as a chipped mug. When Fitz sat facing us on a seat he had to pull down, he told the driver the address in Oak Park, then he introduced us. I murmured politely.

She was slight, and she wore a gray wool coat and dress ensemble with black gloves, hat, and veil. Unlike her court appearance, she had dressed as a fashion plate for this visit. As she sank into the corner, her floral perfume filled the car. She looked out the window. It was a crisp fall day with a bright blue sky. Red, gold, and scratchy brown leaves whipped up in gusts of wind as we rode by.

We drove along in a heavy silence. When I could see we were nearing Oak Park, I turned toward her. "Mrs. Murphy, I wonder if I could ask you a question."

Fitz, who'd been staring at the woman glanced at me warily. Flora Murphy moved her head in my direction, but the veil prevented me from seeing her expression. I plunged ahead before Fitz could object. "Did you know a Miss Caroline Longman? She was Louis Graham's secretary."

Flora's slouching figure straightened and pulled away from me. She turned slightly toward the window in an icy silence. Her gloved hand grasped the door. She watched the street passing by and didn't respond. Why so stiff?

"I wondered if you saw Miss Longman the day that Louis Graham died," I pressed her.

She winced.

Fitz protested. "Mrs. Chapman, Emily, please." His big open hand reached toward me. "Please," he repeated.

I looked him in the eye. "Miss Longman has been missing since Louis Graham's death. People are worried for her safety."

"She can't have been present at the shooting," Fitz protested. "Neither the prosecution nor the defense called on her as a witness. I'm sure she just wanted to avoid the notoriety of the trial by disappearing."

Still no reaction from Flora. Her veil had shivered slightly at Caroline Longman's name, but she didn't deign to speak.

"We're here," Fitz said as we rolled to a stop in front of the huge house with a semi-circular drive. Fitz handed us out and a butler opened the door. With a response that was very different from when I'd come before with Whitbread, the servant stepped aside and welcomed us in.

Fitz glanced at me with doubt, but it was too late for him to detach me, and I was more than ever determined to listen in on the conversation between Flora Murphy and her ailing husband.

THIRTY-NINE

We stepped into a large foyer that was two stories high with a banister around the second floor. Opposite the door, a broad staircase led to a landing and split to separate stairs on each side. The room reminded me of the university public rooms with all the carved wooden paneling, Oriental rugs, and runners. I had visited a few of the neighboring mansions owned by wealthy Hull House donors. The decoration in Big Mike's home was every bit as impressive as what I'd seen, but I doubted those neighbors ever visited. How had they reacted to the owner of saloons, brothels, and gambling dens when he moved to their neighborhood? Not well, I imagined. It must have been a lonely place for Flora Murphy to move to after living in the raucous city.

She removed her coat and hat, handing them to the butler as if she were sleep walking. She wore a long-waisted silk dress with a lace collar that looked almost prim. Her eyes rose to the next floor. Of course she'd entered this house hundreds of times. I suspected she missed it. I sensed apprehension in her as I declined to give my own coat and hat to the butler. I wanted to be free to leave if I felt so inclined. Fitz also waved the man off.

Before we could move to the staircase, a woman hurried from an adjoining room and mounted three steps, then turned to face us. White haired, in a black serge dress that would have served for a funeral, she was Big Mike's first wife, Eileen Murphy. Her son, Malcolm, followed her with a worried look on his face. "Mother, you must let her go up. He wants to see her." He put an arm around her shoulders trying to lead her away.

"How dare she?" Eileen mumbled. "After all that she's done. How dare she? I want to see him. I should be at his side, not her."

I could hear Malcolm try to hush her as I followed Fitz and Flora. We brushed past the upset woman to climb the stairs.

At the top, we entered a sizable bedroom, but the air was close and stale. There was a young man all in black with a Roman collar saying a rosary at the bedside. As Fitz ushered Flora in, the priest gave up his seat and left. I could hear him murmuring outside and knew he was preventing Eileen Murphy from entering. Fitz led Flora to the chair by the bedside and pulled up two more for himself and me. We were behind her in the shadows. Mike Murphy's skin was white, and his flesh hung from his face like a collapsed balloon. He seemed to have shrunk. Was it only a week before that I had seen him in his office, fit for man of his age? I wondered if he had suffered a stroke. His once powerful shoulders sank into a pile of pillows. A doctor with a stethoscope stood by a bureau top laid out with instruments and medications. I could hear harsh breaths going in and out of Big Mike's open mouth. The saloon keeper was clearly not long for the world.

Flora slumped in the chair. Big Mike's eyes opened, and he just stared at her. At that, she broke down into sobs, dropping her head to the blanket, mumbling that she was sorry. He moved a clumsy paw to the top of her head, as if to comfort her. Was he forgiving her?

"Oh, Pa, I'm so sorry. I didn't mean it." Tears stained Flora's carefully made-up face.

"It's all right, Baby. You'll be all right. I took care of you, don't worry." She kissed his hand. He closed his eyes. But in a minute, he opened them again. "Fitz."

Fitz rose to step behind her chair and held on to it. "I'm here."

"She didn't do it." It was hard for Big Mike to talk. He tried to glare at the politician.

Fitz just shook his head, but this was my chance to find out what really happened, so I spoke up. "Who did, Mike? Did you send someone?"

"She didn't."

"Who shot Louis Graham?" I asked. "The typist is still missing. Where is she? You don't want to go with that on your conscience now, do you? Where is Caroline Longman? Is she still alive?"

Mike opened his eyes, but they were groggy. He frowned. I could see the strain of the effort as his forehead wrinkled. But it was too much for him. His breath rattled. The doctor pushed Fitz aside and bent over the man. He murmured to a nurse who appeared beside me, and I moved out of the way as she left the room, returning with the priest. He rubbed oil on the sick man's forehead as the doctor started putting instruments into a bag as if to avoid making a pronouncement. Flora collapsed on the side of the bed in a storm of sobs. I looked at Fitz and together we quietly left the room.

At the threshold, Eileen Murphy pushed past us. She dragged a chair to the foot of the bed. Not to be outdone by Flora, she too began to weep as the priest softly chanted prayers in Latin. In the doorway Malcolm Murphy stood helpless.

Fitz led me down the staircase and Malcolm followed like a pet dog missing its owner.

I wasn't going to get any more information from Flora or Big Mike. The tears rolling down Fitz's cheeks annoyed me. I retrieved the satchel I'd left on the hall table and turned to him. "I don't think you need me anymore. I'll have the butler call me a taxi."

Fitz looked penitent. "I could have my driver take you home. I have to wait for..." He looked up the stairs.

"It's not necessary," I said. "In any case, I need to go to Whitbread at the station." I held up the satchel. "I promised to give him the account book that Agnes Graham found. It proves that her brother was *not* stealing funds from the Liberty Bond drive." Both Fitz and Malcolm looked uncomfortable. I purposely wanted to remind them of Louis Graham, who had died because of the actions of Big Mike and Flora. My sympathy for either of them was sorely limited.

"The trial is over," Fitz said.

"I know that, but Agnes is fighting for her life and if it will make her feel better that the police have this evidence, it's the least we can do for her. She wants to restore her brother's reputation. He was not a thief." I purposely flaunted the account book to make Malcolm remember that he was the one who'd accused the dead man of stealing.

Fitz glanced at my satchel with a sheepish look. Then he looked around uneasily as if he knew the root of the tragedy for the Graham family was in this house. I thought of the scene above. Mike Murphy slipping away with the two women who'd betrayed him begging forgiveness. Or were they weeping for themselves, since the sole audience for their emotional gyrations was going where they would no longer be able to reach him? The mansion seemed a huge cold sepulcher for the dying man. Big Mike Murphy had looked at home in the smoky office above his saloon. Here, he seemed a shrunken skeleton of himself. I felt suffocated by the chilly selfish feelings of this family, and I needed to get away.

Malcolm Murphy stepped up to me. "Mrs. Chapman, let me drive you into the city. My motor is here."

I was angry with Malcolm, too. His testimony had maligned Louis Graham and my daughter. Yet I pitied him. How could he have turned out any better growing up in a home with such parents? In any case, I didn't want his company. "Thank you, Malcolm, but I think you need to stay here. Your father is failing."

His face flushed. "I have errands to do," he said harshly. His eyes rolled toward the ceiling. "They're for *him*. God help me if I don't get them done." He shook himself. "In any case, I have to go into the city, please let me take you."

His father was dying but it seemed the young man wanted to escape this house as much as I did. "All right," I said. "Thank you."

FORTY

Malcolm dismissed his driver after the man started the car. He wanted to drive himself, so he left the driver behind. Instead, Malcolm helped me into the front seat. I held my satchel on my lap. The back of the car was filled with crates. Presumably delivering them was the errand for his father.

When we pulled away from the mansion, I could see the young man relax. As he shifted the gears of the car, his breathing slowed. He probably felt in charge of all the power of the big car.

I waited until we were on a straight stretch of road to ask a question. "Malcolm, you were at the Monadnock Building the day Louis Graham was shot. Did your stepmother really shoot him?"

He glanced at me and shrugged. "When I got down there, she was on the sofa, he was lying on the ground with the pistol beside him." He concentrated on the road.

He wouldn't tell me if one of his father's henchmen had been there. He was loyal to his father. "Did you see Louis Graham's secretary, Caroline Longman?"

"His secretary?" Malcolm's brow furrowed. "I don't remember seeing her." He glanced across at me with a doubtful look. "She was very friendly with Jack Jones and his men," he said.

"What do you mean?"

"Caroline Longman used to go to the Dil Pickle. I think she was involved with the Wobblies up there. I had that impression anyhow."

What did that mean about her absence? Had the IWW men taken her? Or was she hiding out with them? I would tell Whitbread about this detail when I saw him. "But you didn't see her the day Louis Graham was killed?"

"No. People rushed in from the other offices. I picked up the gun from the floor, and Flora kept weeping. Of course, she always faints when she gets in trouble. I wish I could get away with that."

"You testified against her at the trial, didn't you? Was your father angry about that?"

"Yeah, sure. I always get the blame. You wouldn't believe what he did for Louis. He set him up with his own company, you know. Do you think he would do that for his own son? No, always the gofer, that's me. He kept Louis from the draft, sent him out to California, set him up in business when he came back. All to try to keep him away from Flora. They were betraying him, and all he did was try to bribe them. Both of them." He hit the steering wheel with his right hand.

"It must have been difficult for you."

"Oh, well, the sins of the mother get visited upon the son. My own mother wasn't exactly faithful."

It must have been a difficult situation for a young boy, growing up in such turmoil.

We came to an intersection, and he asked. "Is it the Harrison Street station you want to go to?" He glanced at me.

"Actually, I'd like to go to the Art Institute, if you could take me. I can visit Detective Whitbread later." I sighed as I smoothed the leather satchel in my lap. It wouldn't save Louis Graham's reputation. I would deliver the account book to keep Jack's promise to Agnes, but there was no hurry. It was too late for Whitbread to do anything with it. I thought the detective would want to know about Caroline Longman's connection to the IWW men, but I was more worried about Lizzie's search for something among Agnes's belongings. I was also uneasy about Lizzie's concern for Eli Lieberman. That reminded me how much my daughter's reputation was threatened by the trial. "Malcolm, were you there when Flora Murphy made a scene in a restaurant about Louis and Lizzie?"

He pulled his eyes from the road to give me a guilty glance. He swallowed. "Lizzie wasn't involved with Louis. His sister just tried to get him away from Flora's influence. She was the one who arranged for Louis to take Lizzie places." Malcolm sounded resentful. "And she never told Lizzie about Louis and Flora. I finally told Jack. It wasn't right. She needed to know Louis was involved with Flora from when he was sixteen. They couldn't keep away from each other. No matter what Agnes or his mother or my father did. They drew each other like magnets. Flora saw him with Lizzie and she made a scene."

He pulled up in front of the Art Institute and jumped out to come around and help me. I thanked him.

"If my father had just let Louis go fend for himself none of this would have happened," he told me. "If Louis were penniless, Flora would've dropped him. I know it. But *Big Mike* wouldn't let it go. He wouldn't let *her* go. Even after all of this, he's giving her everything. It isn't fair."

It sounded like a plea. I couldn't help him. I felt sorry for him, playing delivery boy for his father even when the man lay on his deathbed. How awful that the father spurned a son who admired him so much.

I took a breath and climbed the stairs between the stone lions. Life wasn't fair but Malcolm Murphy was alive. The same couldn't be said for Louis Graham, Frank Cervone, and perhaps Caroline Longman. And Agnes Graham was hanging on by a thread as fine as a spider's web.

FORTY-ONE

T he Art Institute was busier on a weekday than on Saturday, so I waited in line and purchased a ticket. I had to wait again when a troop of young men and a few women came up the stairs from the studio area. They carried large sketchpads. Lizzie had told me that classes would sit for hours in galleries copying old masters. I scanned the young faces but didn't see my daughter.

As I waited, my mind tumbled over what Malcolm had told me. Could Caroline Longman be hiding with the IWW agitators? Agnes Graham had disappeared that first night at the Dil Pickle. Could she have seen or heard something that made her a danger to the men or their plot? Was that why she'd been shot? Lizzie had come to look for evidence among Agnes's things, but what if it was what she had *seen* that was the problem? And if Agnes had seen something what about Jack? Could he be in danger too? I was uneasy. Lizzie and I should go and find Jack.

Downstairs the corridor was quiet, with light shining from a couple of doorways. Most of the students must have gone off to sketch. As I hurried along, I heard a noise behind me, and looking back, I saw a door close at the far end. Perhaps one of the students had forgotten something.

In Agnes Graham's studio area, I found Lizzie with a large leather portfolio spread out on the floor. She was standing before an unframed canvas propped up on an easel. It depicted the face of a young man in shades of blue. But you didn't see the face at first because it was broken apart into different sized squares as if a drawing had been cut up and thrown down. It was only when I stared for a minute that the portrait resolved into that of an unhappy young man. Somehow the broken pieces of his face demonstrated an underlying agony that was denied by a smile on the lips. It certainly held my attention.

"How very strange," I said, resting my satchel on a table.

"Mother, you're here." Lizzie watched my face as I stared at the picture. "It's a portrait Agnes did of Louis."

"But..."

"I know, it looks strange to you. It's in a style called Cubism. It's too modern for the institute, that's why it's for the unsanctioned exhibit. I'm trying to decide if Agnes would want to show it or if it's too personal."

"Are all the works so modern?" I asked.

Lizzie laughed. "Yes. That's the point. You must remember the Armory exhibit from a couple of years ago? The one that came in from New York and was so explosive?"

I vaguely recalled outraged news stories about the types of paintings and sculptures shown, but I hadn't attended.

"It's where the real work is being done. It's where art is going in the future," Lizzie said. "You know when Miss

Cassatt first exhibited her paintings they were disdained just as much as this."

I always thought that Lizzie's visit with the famous artist during our trip to Paris in 1900 inspired her own desire to be a sculptor.

"I see." I didn't really, but it wasn't my area of expertise. "Did you find anything to explain who shot Agnes, or why?"

She sighed. "No. But I know there was something. Agnes became very secretive in the past week. There was something she was hiding. I think Jack knows what it is."

"I'm afraid he might be a target, too. I think we should go find him at the hospital and make him tell us."

"What's that? Do you smell something?" Lizzie asked.

"Smoke." The art venues Lizzie inhabited were always tinged with the smell of paints and linseed oil, but a little drift of smoke came in the door and the acrid scent of burning tickled my nose.

"Oh, no. That's a fire." Lizzie hurried out the door and I followed her. We rushed down the corridor, coughing as we got closer to the door at the end. Two other women appeared from a side corridor. Lizzie waved at them. "It's a fire, get help." She coughed as she entered the room that was thick with smoke, and she looked around. Though my eyes were watering, I could see a metal basket with dirty rags draped over the side. It was aflame.

"Lizzie, come on, let's get out," I yelled.

She grabbed a canvas tarp that she threw over the fire. I turned and rushed back the way we had come. At the archway to the stairs up and out, I hesitated. I thought of the portfolio of Agnes's work that Lizzie said meant so much to her. The smoke wasn't as thick down the hall

where I saw the doorway to Agnes's area. We should leave
the building and call for the firemen. Knowing I shouldn't,
I ran down the hallway and turned into Agnes's room. In
my mind I could hear Stephen and Lizzie scolding me for
turning back, but Agnes had lost so much recently.

From the doorway, I saw figure stooped over a table.
He was pulling papers out of my satchel. It was Malcolm
Murphy.

FORTY-TWO

I coughed and he looked up. "What are you doing, Malcolm?"

He jumped at my voice. His face scrunched up in a pained grimace, he pointed a pistol at me.

"No," I said, raising my hands to ward him off. He was wild-eyed. I was afraid he'd fire at me by mistake. "Stop, Malcolm."

He trembled, swallowed, and said, "Come in and shut the door. Quick!" The gun wavered dangerously in his hand.

I stepped inside, staring down the muzzle of his gun. "Malcolm, please. There's a fire, we need to get out of here."

He gaped. "No. Shut the door." All the while he rummaged in my satchel with his left hand. His gaze darted from me to the papers. I pulled the door shut behind me and leaned against it.

"The account book. Is that what you want?" I asked, hoping to distract him. He dug down and pulled out the black leather-bound book, hugging it to his chest as his right hand shook with the heavy gun.

"You should have left with Lizzie," he said. He stood as if not seeing me. He was a creature backed into a corner and he would attack any moment. I couldn't believe it. I barely recognized him as the young man who had so courteously driven me that morning was going to shoot me. He was shaking and he certainly wasn't rational. There was no time for discussion.

I felt the doorknob in the small of my back and slipped a hand behind me. I turned the knob and dropped down, scurrying through the door and into the corridor.

A shot burst after me, splintering the heavy door. I turned my knee getting up, but I jumped and ran toward the smoke. Behind me, I heard him cough. He was a madman. I found the wall and felt my way to the archway with the stairs up to the entrance.

"Mother!" I heard Lizzie call as she came down the stairs looking for me.

"No, Lizzie, get back." A shot went off and chipped the stone wall. "Stop it, Malcolm," I yelled again. I heard his footsteps and cough behind me. There was no logic to his actions. What would he gain by shooting me? I'd thought he cared for Lizzie, but nothing would stop him now from shooting her as well, and the thought of bullets ricocheting around the stone walls terrified me.

Furious at the young man's stupidity, I turned on him and threw out an arm to slap him in the face. "Malcolm, stop it," I screamed. It was a crazy thing to do, but I couldn't let him get to Lizzie. And somehow I thought I could do something to snap him out of it.

My daughter barreled down the stairs, coughing, and grabbed Malcolm's arm just as the gun went off again.

Lizzie was as wild as I was. Then we were all three on the floor. What else could we do?

The impact knocked the gun out of Malcolm's hand. Seeing it through my watering eyes, I slid across and grabbed it then turned in a crouch and yelled at him. "Stop, Malcolm, or I'll shoot. Don't think I won't. I know how to shoot a gun." Detective Whitbread had been my teacher and I was a pretty good shot.

Lizzie pulled away from him and he sat up, weeping, whether from the smoke or frustration, I couldn't tell. He still clutched the account book to his breast but he was broken. Just then two big firemen hustled down the stairs, carrying axes, and jingling with other tools hanging from their belts. They refused to listen to explanations, lifting us up and dragging us to the foyer where the door stood open and other men hurried through to go downstairs. I plunged the revolver into my pocket. There was no time for explanations.

They deposited us outside, away from the door. One of the firemen heard my request for the police and sent on the message. When a patrolman arrived, I convinced him to alert Detective Whitbread. When he left, I kept the pistol grimly pointing at Malcolm Murphy, but he had lost all fight and sat on the ground with his head in his hands.

The fireman worked on putting out the blaze while we remained just inside on the steps, gulping fresh air. Lizzie finished coughing and sat on a stone bench staring at Malcolm. "Whatever were you doing here with a gun?" she asked him.

He groaned but didn't raise his head. I bent down, gun in my right hand, and pulled the leather-bound book from his arms. "He was looking for this, the accounts that proved Louis Graham didn't steal money from the Liberty Bond drive," I said. "You were the one doing the stealing, weren't you, Malcolm?" I shook my head. "Malcolm was the one with the gambling problem, weren't you, Malcolm?"

I balanced the book against my waist and ruffled through it, but I had no idea what the figures meant. I handed it to Lizzie.

"Malcolm, you were going to shoot my mother just to hide the figures in this book?" Lizzie asked.

"He shot Agnes for the same reason," I told her grimly.

"I couldn't let her tell my pa," Malcolm said. "He would disown me. He always favored Louis. He let *her* get away with anything." He meant his stepmother, Flora. "I couldn't let Agnes give that book to my father; he'd know what I did. He'd disown me. He'd leave me nothing. He already disinherited my mother. We'd have nothing."

I realized something. "Frank Cervone was with you at the Dil Pickle because you owed money and he was trying to get it from you, wasn't he?"

"It wasn't Eli he was looking for," Lizzie said. She sat up and glared at Malcolm, who leaned his back against the wall and drew up his knees.

"I'll bet you're the witness who claimed you saw Dr. Lieberman with a gun that night," I said. "You were the one who shot Cervone, weren't you?"

"He wouldn't leave me alone. I told him I'd get the money, but he was going to my father, and I couldn't let him do that."

I thought of the crates in Malcolm's motorcar. "And the guns. You weren't at the Dil Pickle to become a partner;

you were selling guns to Jack Jones for the IWW. That was your father's business with them, selling guns. He wasn't going to buy the Dil."

He hung his head, not denying it.

I wondered if Malcolm was the one who'd shot Louis. Had he done it for his father? But why wouldn't Flora have accused him? Fear of Big Mike? Before I could ask, Detective Whitbread arrived with his men. I tried to tell him what had happened with Malcolm and how he was the one who'd shot Cervone and Agnes. Lizzie tried to interrupt to demand he release Eli Lieberman. Whitbread waved away our explanations.

"Don't worry. I'll take Mr. Murphy into custody and straighten this out. But you must go to your husband at Cook County. My car is outside, and my driver will take you." At our puzzled expressions he looked grim. "It's Stephen, Emily. He's very ill and your son sent word that you need to come immediately."

FORTY-THREE

The bells clanged and an alarm roared as we raced to Cook County Hospital. I grasped Lizzie's hand. Stephen must be in a bad way for the police to rush us off like this.

At the hospital desk a nurse quickly led us away. As I followed, I realized we were heading to the basement and my heart sank in my breast. The morgue. Oh, no. I was nearly running by the time we reached the corridor still lined with sheeted bodies. Oh, Stephen, no.

Jack stepped out of Eli's office at the end of the corridor and ran toward us. I was so choked up I couldn't even ask. "No," he said. "He's not gone. There was no room in the ward, so we moved him down here to Eli's office." He grabbed my hand and pulled me down to the doorway.

Stephen lay on a mattress placed on top of the broad table. He was propped up with pillows, and a tall stool was by his side. I ran to him, reaching out for his hand. "Stephen."

He coughed and looked at me with rheumy eyes.

"Papa," Lizzie breathed at my side. He reached out to pat her hand and she gulped back a sob.

"It's all right, Lizzie. There's a good girl." He talked to her as if she were still a child.

Jack came and stood beyond Stephen's pillow. Tears streamed down his face, and he shook his head.

"What happened?" I asked stupidly. I wanted to reach out and stop something with my hands, a useless gesture. It was too late, and that insidious disease would seep through my fingers like water.

Stephen coughed. "I'm afraid it got me." He laid his head back and shut his eyes. "Thought I could beat it. Didn't tell you."

"He's been sick for several days," Jack said. "He didn't want us to know because he was afraid we'd come and get infected. I finally found him yesterday, but he demanded I keep his secret. I'm sorry, Mother. I should have told you."

Stephen waved a hand. "No use," he muttered.

I grabbed his hand. "Oh, Stephen, you should have let us know. I should have insisted on seeing you."

"He'd only let me send for you after we moved him down here when it got so bad." Jack put his hands to his face.

Stephen gathered his strength and opened his brown eyes wide. "Now, now, none of that. There's nothing you could have done." He closed his eyes and breathed heavily.

But there must have been something I could have done. Why didn't I insist he come home nights? I could have stopped him from treating the ill at the first sign of infection. Why had I been running around finding information for Detective Whitbread when I should have been with Stephen? An abyss of might-have-beens opened at my feet and I shivered. I grasped his hand harder. He was slipping away from me.

Lizzie moved past me to lay her head on his chest, and he kissed her hair but weakly pushed her away. "Emily," he whispered. "Infection."

I sighed and pulled her to me. Lizzie was weeping. I patted her back. Stephen's watery eyes stared into mine. "Don't leave us," I said in a breathy whisper.

He relaxed a bit and smiled, then coughed. "Not my choice," he said. "You'll be all right, Em."

"I won't." I was angry. He couldn't leave me like this.

"Sorry," he said and closed his eyes. "You never could take no for an answer, Emily, but this isn't something you can fix, you know."

I remembered all the times I'd argued with him, making him agree with me in the end. I'd insisted he give up his experiments with radiology when it was harming him. I'd gotten him to forgive his father before the man died. I'd convinced him to help our wayward son, Tommy, in the end. Really it was because Stephen was a kind man, even if he was astute enough to see the bad where I had too much sympathy. I silently cursed myself for not making him stop working in the flu wards, but I knew I wouldn't have succeeded this time. I wished I could breathe in the infection and follow him where he was going. I was afraid to stay without him.

He guessed my thoughts. "They need you, Emily." He waved a hand weakly at Lizzie and Jack.

I thought of the Dil Pickle and Lizzie defending Eli Lieberman, Jack's anguish over Agnes Graham's condition. So many things I needed to tell Stephen, to get his opinion about, to get his help. I felt a panicky flutter in my chest. I needed Stephen, sitting at his desk in his cozy study making pithy comments on our children's troubles as I described them. How could I go on if he wasn't there?

It wasn't fair. He wouldn't see our children grow and marry and have children of their own. He was a good man. After all his work to help in this horrid epidemic, he didn't deserve to have his future taken away from him.

"Stephen, I love you," I said, breaking down to weep.

"Dearest Emily," he whispered. "My love." I felt the pressure of his hand in mine, and I looked down at it, then his touch fell away. I looked up in panic at his face. His eyes glazed over, there was a final rattle of breath, and his body went slack.

Lizzie and Jack both looked on with horror. Lizzie pulled away from me. Jack turned away, doubling over. They wept.

I bent forward to kiss his cheek. Then I moved the stool closer and took his hand, bending my head to the blanket and wept.

Forty-Four

I stayed with him all day and all night. I didn't have the energy to move anywhere else. Jack and Lizzie were in and out, bringing me hot tea, but I couldn't eat anything. I had an idea if I just stayed there I could will him back to life, foolish idea. Stephen would have chuckled at my stupidity. But I didn't have him to nudge me out of my beliefs. I finally fell asleep sitting on the stool halfway across the room from him. I longed to lie with him, but I knew he would hate for us to risk infection. We even put on our masks again, knowing he would want it.

In the morning, I sat up stiffly. Stephen wasn't there. His body was there, but it was cold and stiff. As I raised my head and realized where I was, a piece of me broke off and crumbled to dust. I was lighter, as if a weight had fallen away, but it exposed a huge sore wound to the air. I moved painfully.

Lizzie brought me more tea. She was frowning, tears dropping down her cheeks. Jack stood at the door arguing with a man who looked like a hospital porter. When he saw

I was awake, he came in, the bulky man at his heels. "I'm sorry, ma'am, but we must move the body."

Body? I looked at Stephen's husk. Is that what it was?

"No," Jack said. "You need to wait for the coffin."

"There's none left these days," the man said kindly. "Like as not he'll have to be buried in the shroud like the rest of 'em." He waved toward the corridor. "There's not been no coffins for days now. I'm sorry but we has to move them. It's the law like."

I stared at him without taking it all in. He wanted to just bundle Stephen away with the other dead bodies and plant him somewhere in a group grave? How could he do that? I'd seen them carrying out bodies, but I'd hadn't imagined what they did with them after that.

Jack's face was ruddy with rising anger. I wanted to calm him down, but I felt paralyzed, almost as if I saw Jack and Lizzie and the porter through a glass window.

There was a movement in the doorway, and we all turned toward it. Fitz came lumbering in followed by Detective Whitbread. Seeing Stephen, they removed their hats.

"Emily, I'm so sorry," Fitz said. "Whitey here found me and told me. He's gone, is he?" He stepped up and looked down at Stephen. They hadn't always agreed on things, but I knew Stephen had a soft spot for Fitz. And Fitz respected my husband, and I always thought he was even a bit afraid of him. "He was a good man and a great doctor. He'll be sorely missed." Fitz hung his head.

Whitbread stood up straight. "It's a great loss to all of us," he said. He and Stephen had respected each other and shared an exasperation over my actions at times. Whitbread and his wife were true friends of ours.

Fitz said. "I've contacted Maloney's funeral home. They'll be by any time now with a coffin."

The porter said, "You won't be needing me then. Just so's you got him out of here by end of day."

Jack took him by the shoulder and firmly led him away.

Tears choked my throat with relief when I tried to thank Fitz. He saw that and pulled me in an embrace so I could weep on his broad shoulder. "I'm so sorry, Emily. But there'll be a small service at the university chapel tomorrow."

I pulled back and looked at him with disbelief. Funerals were forbidden due to the flu.

"It's just a small gathering for two other university folks who passed this week. It'll be done really quietly."

I looked at Stephen with doubt. How would he feel about ignoring the restrictions?

"It's not for him so much as for you and your children," Fitz said. "He'll not be objecting now, and you'll be needing it."

The thought ran through my mind that Fitz spent a considerable amount of time visiting the funerals of his constituents. It had always been one of his duties. I supposed it made him an expert in this sort of thing.

"Your husband would wish you to do whatever comforts you," Whitbread interjected. I knew his opinion echoed what Stephen would think.

"Thank you," I told Fitz.

FORTY-FIVE

W hen the Armistice was signed on November 11, ending the war, Chicago went crazy. Despite continued infection, the city had dropped all flu restrictions on November 4, just as Fitz had promised. Stephen would have been furious. The wiser among us still wore masks and avoided public gatherings. But that was impossible the day that peace was finally declared.

By then I was trying to crawl back out of my sorrow. It was more than a week since we'd laid Stephen in the ground next to a stone plaque engraved with the name of our dead son, Tommy. There was a sickly silence in our townhouse, and I avoided Stephen's study. Jack and Lizzie both returned home in the evenings and tried to comfort me.

That day I had to get out of the house. My son Jack had confessed to me about what he and Agnes had been up to. I needed to tell Whitbread, so I convinced Jack to come with me to Whitbread's office. We fought our way through crowds to reach the Harrison Street station. Men and women bursting with joy around me sang "Star

Spangled Banner," "America," and "Over There" in every street. We saw women as well as men toasting the end of the war to end all wars through the open doors of the saloons.

We saw men dressed as harlequins, motorcars with little figures of the Kaiser on their hoods. People battered other effigies of the German leader with rotten tomatoes, sticks, and stones. We came across a crowd gathered around two men fighting, and I was pushed to a wall by the movement until a young woman rushed up, put her arms around the men and gave each a big kiss. The crowd applauded. Jack and I hurried away. The demonstrations on November 11 were spontaneous, widespread, and unavoidable. As if a dam had broken.

When we finally reached the door of the police station, a uniformed man let us in. Upstairs my students had moved to a room with windows on the street to view the wild crowds below. I learned that people had arrived at work all over the city only to be dismissed by their employers to celebrate the peace. Whitbread was out with the rest of the police force trying to prevent havoc. I sat at his desk and Jack sat opposite me.

Of course, I was glad the nightmare of the war was finally over. And the epidemic had receded despite the lax enforcement of preventive measures. Certainly, there was no keeping people away from each other on a day like this.

I found it hard to share the exhilaration. Although my son and daughter had returned to our home in Hyde Park to comfort me after Stephen's death, the situation of my family seemed precarious. I wasn't sure if Lizzie was seeing Eli Lieberman or not. He'd been released when Whitbread arrested Malcolm Murphy, and he attended Stephen's funeral. But Lizzie barely mentioned him, and Jack was silent about his friend. They knew I disliked his influence on them. Lizzie was waiting for her mentor, Lorenzo Taft, to return to put together all the pieces of his sculpture on the Midway.

Agnes Graham had not been well enough to attend the funeral and I worried about her relationship with Jack. She'd been released from the hospital to her home in Oak Park, but when I suggested we go and visit her, Jack put me off. When I insisted, he finally told me the secret he and Agnes had been keeping.

Detective Whitbread hurried through the door. "Emily, how are you? Dr. Chapman." He nodded at Jack.

I hadn't seen the detective since Stephen's funeral. "I'm fine. You must thank Gracie again for all of her help." Recovered from her recent bout with the flu, Whitbread's wife had come and taken over the house after my husband's death. She'd stayed a week with us, preparing meals, cleaning, and organizing the post-funeral gathering.

"Anything you need, you have only to ask," he said. He took off his hat and tossed it on a file cabinet. "There is an animal exuberance to the celebrations today. We need to prevent the crowds from cheering themselves to death out there. But restraint is hopeless." He motioned for me to keep the seat behind his desk and dropped into a hard chair opposite me.

"What happened to Malcolm Murphy?" I asked. "I lost track..." I didn't have to explain my preoccupation with the loss of Stephen.

"He'll plead guilty. He was contrite after the shooting at the museum. I think he was shocked at his own actions. He had no intention to hurt you or your daughter. Then, after his father's death he completely fell apart."

"Big Mike Murphy died?"

"Yes. And despite the regulations there was a funeral procession of twenty automobiles." He shook his head. "Fitz arranged it. He convinced me to allow the son to attend. Everything Malcolm Murphy did was to impress his father. With that audience gone, he collapsed. Big Mike left Flora well off and he left the house in Bridgeport to Malcolm's mother, but he left nothing for his son. He knew about the gambling and the debts. He was disgusted with Malcolm. That's why the boy was so desperate to keep his stealing the Liberty Bond money secret."

"Did Malcolm admit he shot Frank Cervone and Agnes?" I asked.

"Frank Cervone and Miss Graham, but he still claims Flora shot Louis." Whitbread shrugged. I glanced at Jack.

"And the theft of the Liberty Bond money?"

"He admits he was the one who took it. He says he just found it convenient to blame Louis when he was dead. We found the crates of guns in his automobile, and he admitted to his plans to sell them for his father. All that talk about buying an interest in the Dil Pickle was just negotiations to buy the guns and ammunition. Jones was stalling because he lacked money. But we didn't have enough to charge Jack Jones and his crew since Malcolm didn't deliver the merchandise. They've calmed down in any case. Did you hear about Bill Haywood?"

"No, what happened?"

"He skipped bail to run off to Russia. He defected. That took the wind out of the sails for the IWW demonstration. They've condemned him as a coward and a traitor. It's a good thing they didn't get their hands on all those guns anyhow."

I was glad to hear there would be no violent insurrection over the sentencing.

There was no sense waiting any longer. "Jack has something to tell you about Caroline Longman," I said. "She's alive and well."

Whitbread's eyebrows went up and he turned his sharp gaze on my son.

Jack swallowed. "I'm sorry we kept it from you so long, but Caroline Longman was involved with Louis and is carrying his child. Agnes and Mrs. Graham have taken her in and will help her."

Whitbread whistled. Then he turned his chair to face Jack. "This I must hear. What happened to the young woman?"

Jack frowned. Taking a large breath, he told the story. Caroline Longman had been seeing Louis Graham in secret. Louis was afraid of what Flora Murphy would do if she knew of their relationship. But when Caroline became pregnant, he decided to finally break with Flora and go to Big Mike for help. He told Flora that fateful day. She had already sensed him pulling away and was jealous. She came to the office and, when he told her his plans to marry Caroline and have the child, she pulled out the gun. Caroline had seen him on his knees before his lover, begging for her to let him go, and had seen Flora shoot him. Fearing for her own life, she fled, taking the account book which Louis had told her proved Malcolm Murphy had stolen Liberty Bond funds.

"She ran to her family in Wisconsin," Jack told us. "But they threw her out. She had just returned to Chicago when Agnes spotted her at the Dil Pickle that night that we took you there, Mother. She foolishly thought she could get money from Malcolm by telling him she had the account books. He threatened her. Agnes convinced her to stay with a friend."

"I took my pistol to her for her protection. That's why I didn't have it," he told Whitbread who was nodding. "It was only halfway through the trial, when Agnes had convinced her mother to take Caroline in, that she gave Agnes the account books. Agnes is sure that Louis meant to marry her, and her child will be Louis's child. They plan to treat her as his widow."

"But why didn't she speak up? Her testimony could have gotten Flora Murphy convicted," Whitbread said.

Jack shook his head. "I know. I tried to tell them that, but Mrs. Graham was mortified that Caroline would be presented as an unwed woman carrying a child at the public trial. Agnes and her mother decided that vengeance against Flora meant less to them than protecting his widow and child from public disgrace."

Whitbread grunted in disgust. "But Miss Longman is safe and sound then?"

"Yes. And Mrs. Graham will support her."

"I'm sorry I couldn't tell you sooner, but Agnes made me promise. I only managed to convince her that you should know the truth today. She believes it's much better to help Caroline to have the child quietly and to make sure she and the baby lack nothing. Flora lives but her husband is dead, and her life must surely be destroyed while Agnes's brother will live on a little in his child."

So, Caroline Longman was a witness to the death of Louis Graham after all. But there were no hired killers from Big Mike and the awkward trail the bullet had taken was because Louis had been kneeling before the jealous woman when she shot him. It was a horrible picture and I could understand why Caroline would run to save herself and her baby. I wondered if Big Mike had known what really happened that day.

FORTY-SIX

A week later, I attended the unsanctioned art exhibit that included works by Lizzie and Agnes. Lizzie guided me to a storefront on Wabash beneath the L train a few blocks from the Art Institute. At the door I met the Polish sculptor and his American heiress wife who were hosting the exhibition. He was a tall scarecrow of a man with a heavy accent. She was short and plump. I recognized her from when Lizzie had spent time in Chicago society. Like Lizzie, this young woman had turned her back on all of that for a more bohemian lifestyle.

We moved into the long room. The dark red of the walls contrasted with a white ceiling. Lit by chandeliers and wall sconces that appeared to be fantastical winding leaves, the colors provided a striking backdrop to the sculptures and pictures placed around the room. I spotted Agnes's Cubist portrait of her brother in the middle of the far wall and, closer, I saw a bronze statue that I knew was Lizzie's.

"Oh, Lizzie, it's wonderful," I told her. It was abstract curves of metal. I didn't know how she did it, but I responded at once with the same feelings I'd had when I saw her earlier sculpture of mother and sons in her studio.

"Well, it was quite a project," she said, and I could see her pride peek out from her nonchalance. "I did the study in plaster and then it had to be cast at a factory downtown. It's a small place we've gone in together to support." She waved at someone across the way. "Excuse me, Mother."

My eyes threatened to water as I thought of how proud Stephen would have been of our daughter. I sniffed and wandered down the long room, admiring each painting and sculpture as I passed. I nearly bumped into the reporter Ben Hecht when he backed up and squinted to view one of the Cubist paintings.

"Mrs. Chapman, uh, so sorry to hear of your loss. How are you?" he asked. He looked embarrassed. The last time we spoke I had been so angry at him. But that seemed a long time ago now.

"Mr. Hecht, thank you for your sympathy. I've come to see the work of my daughter and others. I surprised you're not out getting gossip and stories about criminals. Surely this kind of gathering is rather tame for you?" I couldn't help being acerbic.

He blushed. "Actually, I've got a new assignment," he said. "I'm off to Berlin tomorrow." At my raised eyebrows he explained. "They're sending me to report on what's happening in Germany now that they've lost."

He grabbed two glasses from a passing waiter and offered me one.

"To your future endeavors," I toasted him. He still reminded me of my brother, Alden, but I wouldn't be sorry to see him leave the city. We clinked glasses and he swallowed a hearty mouthful while I sipped. "Excuse me," I said. I saw Agnes and Eli planted in the far corner, so I joined them.

"Miss Graham, I'm so happy to see you recovered enough to attend your opening," I told her.

"Please, call me Agnes." She gestured at the wheelchair where she sat. "Lizzie and Eli fixed me up with this." It was an unorthodox version being a brocade upholstered wing chair that was fitted with large and small wheels for movement. Agnes still looked pale and weak, but she wore a sequined hair band and a sequined dress that sparkled when she moved.

I stood between Agnes and Eli looking back at the room. Eli's hair and beard were nicely trimmed, and his suit was well pressed, his shoes shined. He hesitated at a waiter's offer but waved away the champagne. I wondered if Lizzie had lectured him on drink. I followed his eyes as they picked out my daughter in a crowd of her friends. Lizzie wore black, as did I. But her frock had a chiffon overskirt heavily beaded with jet. It rippled when she moved.

I noticed Eli swallow with discomfort and work his finger around his collar. Young society people surrounded Lizzie. They were the sort of people she had spent so much time with before she'd broken off an engagement the year before. Chicago society was amply represented at the opening, and I even saw a newspaper columnist who covered arts and culture. The press was unavoidable, as always. Lizzie and her friends had gone all out to attract a well-heeled crowd and a well-heeled crowd would always attract the predator press.

Eli moved back and forth on his feet beside me. As we looked down the room, people were seeping in, sipping champagne, wandering, greeting friends. I could understand if it looked to the doctor like a wave was creeping toward us. He tensed and I feared he would fly away to find a back door. I regretted my past doubts about him. He was trying so hard. I grabbed his good left hand.

"Eli don't let this crowd frighten you away," I told him. "Lizzie knows these people, she spent time with them in the past, but she rejected them. She doesn't want to be like them. Don't let them worry you." I had concerns about my daughter's relationship with the older doctor. His experience had damaged him physically and emotionally. But I didn't think it was fair for him to be scared off by Chicago society.

Lizzie came up to us bringing a young couple with her. She blithely introduced them. "And this is Dr. Eli Lieberman, who I've been telling you about. Eli, they're interested in our idea." The woman wore a gown in metallic silver with a pound of diamonds strung around her neck. Her husband wore a tuxedo. I recognized them from one of the many committees formed to help the war effort. Lizzie told them about Eli's work with amputees and how he had come by his own disability on the battlefield. He blushed a bit as she held forth.

I knew what she was doing. Wealthy young people like this wanted to help the men who had fought for us. I recalled that this couple had avoided the husband's draft by a quick marriage. Lizzie was well aware of the niggling guilt they felt when faced by the wounds of those who had fought.

"I'm so excited," my daughter said. "We've lined up two other sculptors here to help with the design, and we've located an empty warehouse we could use for the manufacture." She was talking about her work creating artificial limbs for amputees returning from France. "We can even give the injured men work there, do you see. Oh, look, there are the Matthews, let's get them involved, too." She pointed them to another prosperous couple, firmly put her hand in Eli's arm, and steered her group away. With a glance over her shoulder, she winked at me.

I was glad to see her so enthusiastic about her project. It seemed to me that it was the task of all these young people to pick up the pieces of this broken world after the war's end and the petering out of the flu. They would have to rebuild it and I sensed they had no interest in mirroring the past.

At that moment, a short man with a flourishing mustache and a wide flapping Windsor tie rushed up to Agnes. "Darling," he said. "You made it." He stooped to kiss her on both cheeks. "We were all so worried."

She grinned at him.

"I have something for you," he said. Looking around as if to be sure no one was paying attention, he drew out a rolled sheet of paper, tied with a ribbon. "For you, my dear. Do take a look when no one's around. I slaved over it, I promise you, but if you see anything that needs fixing, just let me know." He looked around again then whispered sharply, "September ninth." He glanced up, saw a passing waiter, and hurried after him to get a flute of champagne.

Agnes smiled at his back. She looked around, grinned at me, then, put her glass on the floor. Gently, hiding her actions, she untied the ribbon and unrolled the paper. I peeked over her shoulder. It was a marriage certificate for Caroline Longman and Louis Graham dated September ninth. "Dennis is such a perfectionist," Agnes murmured. She rolled it back up and tucked it behind her.

"I met Caroline last week," I said.

She stiffened as if prepared for criticism. "I think what you're doing for her is admirable," I hurried to say. She relaxed. "I'm only sorry that her testimony can never be used to convict Mrs. Murphy now. She's been acquitted and no matter what evidence we have she can't be tried again. She's free."

"Flora Murphy," Agnes spat out the words. "Did you see in the paper her latest move? She's going to write her memoirs, turn them into a play and star in it on Broadway. That woman."

"Yes, I did see that. I'm sorry she'll never pay for shooting your brother."

Agnes waved a hand. "That's past. It's a great comfort to my mother to have Caroline with us. They're planning to name the baby Louis if it's a boy or Louise if it's a girl. In time, after the publicity calms down, we'll recognize her as Louis's widow, and she'll just be another young widow like so many from the war. She's staying with us now, but that won't last. She's young. I'm sure she'll marry again, and that's all right." She sighed and looked up at me. "I'm grateful to her. I think Louis finally found a way to free himself of Flora Murphy, and I'm glad he could know that feeling before he died." She looked across to where Jack stood in front of her portrait of her brother. He was talking enthusiastically, and I wondered if he was selling the painting to the small crowd around him.

"Jack has asked me to marry him," Agnes said.

My heart skipped a beat, and I took a breath to recover. He hadn't told me. "I'm so happy for you," I said. "I know Jack cares for you an awful lot."

"And I love him with all my heart," she whispered.

I cleared my throat wondering why this announcement was a shock to me. Did I think it was too soon after Stephen's death? I knew my late husband would scoff at such niceties. "I worry about Jack," I told her. "He hasn't gone back to his profession. I don't know how to help him. He worked so hard to become a doctor, he can't abandon it. I want to tell him he could go into research at the university like his father, but I haven't found the right time to say it."

She was watching him. "He'll never treat the living again. He's going to stay in the morgue. Eli will be returning to his work with amputees and Jack will take over as pathologist."

I was shocked. I felt left out that she was privy to his plans, and I was not. I told myself not to be a ninny. Of course he'd share his plans with her. "Do you think that's wise?" I couldn't help asking. "Working with the dead? After all he's been through."

She looked up at me. "Oh, don't think he's gloomy about it. Not at all. In fact, he's enthusiastic. He says legal medicine is a new field and he's been researching it. He wants to explore it."

I looked at my son across the room. He did seem more relaxed, more contained than he'd been during the difficult months since he returned from the battlefield. It made me glad that he'd found someone in Agnes to help him climb out of the despair in which he was mired. In my own grief over Stephen, I'd missed the change in our son.

"You should be complimented by Jack's new obsession," Agnes told me with a shy look. "He admired his father so much, that's why he became a doctor, I think. But he admires you, too. He's told me about your work with the police over the years. He's proud of you. He says the dead deserve to have the truth of their lives known and that you do that by explaining their deaths when there's a question. He wants to do that, too."

I'd never known what my son thought of my work. I always expected him to follow naturally in his father's footsteps. I could picture Stephen grinning at my future daughter-in-law's analysis and nodding his head in agreement. Perhaps he was right, and Jack really took after me. In any case, we had a rocky road ahead of us. There was so much to repair in our lives, but Jack and Lizzie and I would be able to reach out and steady each other. We had to move forward, there was nowhere else to go.

AFTERWORD

For a long time, I planned to set one of the Emily Cabot Mysteries during the Spanish flu epidemic. I even envisioned her husband's death as part of it. But that was before the COVID 19 pandemic that hit in 2020. Before that disaster, the Spanish flu had seemed like a forgotten piece of history, and many of the Emily Cabot Mysteries highlight some forgotten event or person. It's one of the joys of writing historicals to pick out a fascinating jewel of the past that has been lost in the shadows. When I began the book, that was true, but then COVID struck. Despite the pandemic weariness that developed and the frequent stories about the 1918 epidemic that appeared, I completed the book. I hope readers are not too weary of the topic to read it.

As usual, newspaper articles were most helpful in portraying how people saw the Spanish flu at the time. An original source I used is *A Report on an Epidemic of Influenza in the City of Chicago in the Fall of 1918* by John Dill Robertson. Further research into Robertson turned up the stories about his peculiar ideas about hygiene and his political stance on everything. It was hard to believe his claim that bathing was bad and caused tuberculosis. And his political pressure and appointments of cronies to positions in the sanitarium apparently caused a man's suicide. He seems a very true to life Chicagoan in his predilection for politics.

The Dil Pickle club was a find. The best source about the famous avant-garde gathering place is *The Rise & Fall of the Dil Pickle Club: Chicago's Wild '20's* by Franklin Rosemont with a new introduction by Paul Durika. It was a fascinating place that drew the writers and artists as well as hoboes, Wobblies, professors, and ordinary people. Jack Jones was eventually squeezed out by mobsters and went back to being a printer. I highly recommend the book for more great stories about the place.

When I thought of portraying the artistic life of Chicago in one of the books, of course I thought of *Poetry* magazine and Harriet Monroe. But she did seem a bit staid, despite the radical poetry she published. When I investigated it, I found that writers like Sherwood Anderson, Carl Sandburg, and Max Bodenheim all frequented the Dil where they put on plays by Synge, Chekov, O'Neil, and others. When I mentioned I was putting Dil Pickle into the next book to Richard Reeder of the Cliff Dweller's Club, he asked if Ben Hecht would be in it. Research led me to Hecht's autobiography, *A Child of the Century*, which had great anecdotes about the time, so I had to include him. His famous play *Front Page* takes place in the pressroom of the Chicago criminal courts. I used that location in one of the scenes.

That the artistic life of Chicago was often influenced by labor movements like the IWW in the Dil Pickle is consistent with themes in the other books of the series. I think we forget how those movements have always been part of the American dilemma in our pursuit of happiness for all. I took liberties with dates when I had Bill Haywood defect to Russia during the timeline of my book. It wasn't till the next spring, when out on bail, that the former leader of the IWW ran away to Russia.

The murder of Louis Graham is very roughly based on the real trial of Dora McDonald for the murder of Webster Guerin in 1905. But that was only the kernel for my story set in 1918 with fictional characters Big Mike and Flora Murphy and the son, Malcolm. My editor, Emily Victorson, recommended a 1931 book, *Murder for Love* by Ione Quinby. I didn't use the stories of those women but it has some good examples and describes the trials as well. Flora wasn't the only murderous woman of the time.

Eli Lieberman, Agnes Graham, and Caroline Longman are also all fictional characters. Ben Reitman was very real, and I read his book *Sister of the Road: The Autobiography of Box-Car Bertha.* In it, he describes an underworld of people at the time who had beliefs and opinions I thought first appeared in the 1960's. Not true. Back in the 1920's free love and a hippie-like existence were the life of a minority.

I have at least a couple of more stories to come about Emily and her friends and family. I expect them to be published by Rudiyat Press. I also have a new series set in Boston beginning in 1919 to be published by Level Best

Books. I hope readers will look for the new stories and will enjoy them. Thank you for your readership!

ACKNOWLEDGMENTS

Thank you to my critique group in Cambridge, which includes Leslie Wheeler, Mark Ammons, Cheryl Marceau, and Katherine Fast; and also to my beta readers Stuart Miller, Colleen Farrell and Nikki Flionis. Special thanks to editor Emily Victorson formerly of Allium Press of Chicago.

ALSO BY FRANCES MCNAMARA

Emily Cabot Mysteries

Death at the Fair

The 1893 World's Columbian Exposition provides a vibrant backdrop for this exciting new mystery. Emily Cabot is one of the first women graduate students at the University of Chicago, eager to prove herself in the new field of sociology. While she is busy exploring the Exposition with her family and friends, her colleague, Dr. Stephen Chapman, is accused of murder. Emily sets out to search for the truth behind the crime, but is thwarted by the thieves, corrupt politicians, and gamblers who are ever-present in Chicago. A lynching that occurred in the dead man's past leads Emily to seek the assistance of the black activist Ida B. Wells. Rich with historical details that bring turn-of-the-century Chicago to life, this novel will appeal equally to history buffs and mystery fans.

Death at Hull House

It's Chicago in 1893 and Emily Cabot, an aspiring
sociologist, finds work at Hull House, the famous
settlement established by Jane Addams. There she quickly
becomes involved in the political and social problems of
the immigrant community. But when a man who works for
a sweatshop owner is murdered in the Hull House parlor,
Emily must determine whether one of her colleagues is
responsible, or whether the real reason for the murder is
revenge for a past tragedy in her own family. As a smallpox
epidemic spreads through the impoverished West Side of
Chicago, the very existence of the settlement is threatened
and Emily finds herself in jeopardy from both the deadly
disease and a killer. This is the exciting sequel to Death at
the Fair.

Death at Pullman

A model town at war with itself . . . George Pullman
created an ideal community for his railroad car workers,
complete with every amenity they could want or need.
But when hard economic times hit in 1894, lay-offs follow
and the workers can no longer pay their rent or buy
food at the company store. Starving and desperate, they
turn against their once benevolent employer. Emily Cabot
and her friend Dr. Stephen Chapman bring much needed
food and medical supplies to the town, hoping they
can meet the immediate needs of the workers and keep

them from resorting to violence. But when one young worker-suspected of being a spy-is murdered, and a bomb plot comes to light, Emily must race to discover the truth behind a tangled web of family and company alliances.

Death at Woods Hole

Exhausted after the tumult of the Pullman Strike of 1894, Emily Cabot is looking forward to a restful summer visit to Cape Cod. She has plans to collect "beasties" for the Marine Biological Laboratory, alongside other visiting scientists from the University of Chicago. She also hopes to enjoy romantic clambakes with Dr. Stephen Chapman, although they must keep an important secret from their friends. But her summer takes a dramatic turn when she finds a dead man floating in a fish tank. In order to solve his murder she must first deal with dueling scientists, a testy local sheriff, the theft of a fortune, and uncooperative weather. This fourth book in the Emily Cabot Mysteries series will continue to delight history buffs and mystery lovers alike.

Death at Chinatown

In the summer of 1896, amateur sleuth Emily Cabot meets two young Chinese women who have recently received medical degrees. She is inspired to make an important decision about her own life when she learns about the difficult choices they have made in order to pursue their careers. When one of the women is accused of poisoning a Chinese herbalist, Emily once again finds herself in the midst of a murder investigation. But, before the case can be solved, she must first settle a serious quarrel with her husband, help quell a political uprising, and overcome threats against her family. Timeless issues, such as restrictions on immigration, the conflict between Western and Eastern medicine, and women's struggle to balance family and work, are woven seamlessly throughout this riveting historical mystery. Rich with fascinating details of life in Chicago's original Chinatown, this fifth book in the Emily Cabot Mysteries series will continue to delight history buffs and mystery lovers alike.

Death at the Paris Exposition

In the sixth Emily Cabot Mystery, the intrepid amateur sleuth's journey once again takes her to a world's fair—the Paris Exposition of 1900. Chicago socialite Bertha Palmer has been named the only female U. S. commissioner to the Exposition and she enlists Emily's services as her social secretary. Their visit to the House of Worth for the fitting of a couture gown is interrupted by the theft of Mrs. Palmer's famous pearl necklace. Before that crime can be solved, several young women meet untimely deaths and a member of the Palmer's inner circle is accused of the crimes. As Emily races to clear the family name she encounters jealous society ladies, American heiresses seeking titled European husbands, and more luscious gowns and priceless jewels. Along the way, she takes refuge from the tumult at the country estate of Impressionist painter Mary Cassatt. In between her work and sleuthing, she is able to share the Art Nouveau delights of the

Exposition, and the enduring pleasures of the City of Light, with her husband and their young children.

Death at the Selig Studios

The early summer of 1909 finds Emily Cabot eagerly anticipating a relaxing vacation with her family. Before they can depart, however, she receives news that her brother, Alden, has been involved in a shooting death at the Selig Polyscope silent movie studios on Chicago's northwest side. She races to investigate, along with her friend Detective Henry Whitbread. There they discover a sprawling backlot, complete with ferocious jungle animals and the celluloid cowboys Tom Mix and Broncho Billy. As they dig deeper into the situation, they uncover furtive romantic liaisons between budding movie stars and an attempt by Thomas Edison to maintain his stranglehold over the emerging film industry. Before the intrepid amateur sleuth can clear her brother's name she faces a serious break with the detective; a struggle with her adolescent daughter, who is obsessed with the filming of the original Wizard of Oz movie; and threats upon her own life.

Death on the Homefront

With the United States on the verge of entering World War I, tensions run high in Chicago in the Spring of 1917, and the city simmers with anti-German sentiment mixed with virulent patriotism. Shockingly, amateur sleuth Emily Cabot is present when a young Chicago woman, who is about to make a brilliant society marriage, is murdered. Was her death retaliation for her pacifist activities, or was it linked to her romantic entanglements? Emily has a personal connection to the woman, but she's torn between her determination to solve the murder and her deep need to protect her newly adult children from the realities of a new world. As the country's entry into the war unfolds, Emily watches with trepidation as her sons and daughter make questionable choices about their own futures. Violent worker unrest and the tumultuous arena of automobile racing provide an emotionally charged backdrop for this compelling mystery.

Death in a Time of Spanish Flu
In fall of 1918, while the war is finally ending, the Spanish Flu is rampant in Chicago. Emily's husband is treating patients at Cook County Hospital but her son and daughter have been drawn into a scandalous murder trial of the wife of a local gambling king and ward boss. When Emily accompanies her children to the avantgarde Dil Pickle club a man is found shot do death. She works with Detective Henry Whitbread to save her children by finding the real murderer.

CPSIA information can be obtained
at www.ICGtesting.com
Printed in the USA
JSHW061243170822
29395JS00003B/198